USA TODAY BESTSELLING AUTHOR

NANCY WARREN

BAKER'S COVEN

THE GREAT WITCHES BAKING SHOW
BOOK 2

ISBN: ebook 978-1-928145-71-4

ISBN: print 978-1-928145-70-7

Cover Design by Lou Harper of Cover Affair

INTRODUCTION

Can she bake a winning cake without getting iced?

Competition is hotter than the pre-heated ovens as The Great British Baking Competition moves into cake week. Amateur baker Poppy Wilkinson has a lot to deal with, from learning she has talents she never knew about, to trying to keep cool and bake under pressure.

She's also trying to track down the secrets of her parentage. Meanwhile, she's saved from death by a local Border collie who seems to think she's part of his flock and herds her out of danger. Was it an accident or does someone want her out of the baking competition permanently?

With witches, an energy vortex, an ancient manor house that holds it's secrets tight, Poppy's barely got time to practice her fondant icing, never mind escape from a killer.

Taste this culinary cozy mystery series from USA Today Bestselling author Nancy Warren. Each book is a stand-

alone mystery, though the books are linked. They offer good, clean fun, and, naturally, recipes.

The best way to keep up with new releases and special offers is to join Nancy's newsletter at **nancywarren.net**.

BAKER'S COVEN

CHAPTER 1

The gorgeous rolling green hills of Somerset were achingly beautiful in the golden morning light, but they couldn't hold a candle to the electric glow I felt as I hit the accelerator in my little Renault Clio and Broomewode Hall came into view. It was as magnificent as ever. Home to *The Great British Baking Contest*, the manor house was a Georgian masterpiece. The leaded piping lent the symmetrical windows an air of elegant mystery, and the proud turrets reached up as if to touch the few puffy clouds that interrupted the beckoning blue sky. It was surrounded by perfectly manicured lawns and flowerbeds bursting with a wealth of spring offerings: daffodils, tulips, and hyacinths in colorful abundance. To my left was the vast white calico tent where filming took place, and underneath its solemn awning, the workstations were ready and waiting for the second episode of *The Great British Baking Contest* to begin filming.

I pulled into the parking area behind the pub, which also offered comfortable rooms where we baking contestants were housed during filming. I couldn't believe it had only been five days since I'd driven away from the inn. It had been a weekend of fierce baking competition, sabotage, the murder of my new friend Gerry—and then, to top it all off, the great master baker Elspeth Peach informed me that I was a witch.

And so was she.

To say it was a jaw-dropping weekend would be a gigantic understatement. Mind. Blown.

I'd applied to the show because I'd been searching for clues about my birth parents and thought Broomewode Hall might hold the answers. But last weekend I ended up learning things about myself that I never could've predicted. It turned out that I was a water witch, though I still had almost zero clue as to what that really meant. One of my special powers was seeing ghosts, an oddity I'd lived with all my life but had never been able to share with anyone. But now I could share it with a celebrity baker: Elspeth Peach, someone I'd looked up to from afar but now I thought of as family.

Since then, I'd had a restless week. I mean, a climbing the walls kind of week.

I thought that I'd love being back in my sleepy village near Bath in Somerset, and my cottage, The Olde Bakery, in the break before the next episode was to be filmed. I'd always felt protected by its solid stone walls, flagstone floors, and its charming misshapen rooms. Outside, spring was working her magic and my rambling herb garden was luscious and fragrant. The murderous drama of last weekend's show was behind me, but I couldn't shake the feeling that my home, well, didn't feel so homey anymore.

It was strange. I couldn't quite put my finger on the problem. Everything was as I'd left it. My baking equipment was piled high on the draining board by the sink; the clothes I'd rejected for filming were still scattered across my bed after my last-minute panic packing. Even Mildred, my resident ghost, was there to greet me when I got in, desperate to know how all her baking tips had fared in the competition. My sweet new cat, Gateau, who'd attached herself to me at Broomewode Hall, had no problem making herself comfy immediately. It took her all of ten minutes to adjust to her new surroundings. She sniffed about the place and then settled on the armchair in front of the kitchen's fireplace, the spot where I usually sat and trawled through recipe books. But being away from Broomewode Hall felt—wrong. I couldn't shake the sensation that I needed to be back there.

I tried to ignore the pull and spent as much time as I could practicing for the coming weekend's cake challenge. One evening I had Gina over to taste-test my cakes as well as share some Chinese takeout, a bottle of wine, and indulge in a *Friends* marathon.

It was so nice for us to spend some girly time together after all that happened and try to decompress, but even these pleasures didn't overcome the odd feeling that continued to plague me. Besides, Gina still couldn't get her head around the incident in the forest when Gordon was trying to kill her and I had a huge power surge that seemed to come out of nowhere and managed to throw him off her. I couldn't convince Gina to drop the subject, so instead I plied her with egg rolls until she became too full to ask any more questions. Blessed be the egg roll.

When I suspected the whole of last weekend had been an elaborate nightmare, and I wasn't a contestant on the long-running reality show at all, I'd touch the amethyst necklace that Elspeth had given me for protection. Every time I touched the beautiful purple stone, I felt calmer.

According to Elspeth, I was connected to a coven of witches. Witches! I'd kept my eyes open for pointy hats, warts on noses, boiling cauldrons and broom-shaped flying objects, but Broomewode and the connected village seemed tranquil. I was more likely to come across grazing sheep and friendly villagers than witches. Or so I hoped.

Still, after a couple of days at home, I could no longer ignore the urge to get back to Broomewode Hall. I remembered what Elspeth said when she first told me I was a witch: *Settle your mind and don't ignore your intuition.* I knew that several things were bothering me.

First, I was desperate to continue searching for information about my birth parents. As a baby, I'd been left in an apple crate outside the Philpott's bakery in Norton St. Philip, a charming village near Bath in Somerset. I had zero information about my parents. The only clue was the hand-knitted baby blanket I'd been bundled in. I'd seen an identical design on a shawl draped across a woman in a painting at Broomewode Hall when I'd been watching the show.

Rumor had it that a mystic energy ran from Glastonbury, where King Arthur is said to be buried, to Broomewode Hall and beyond. Elspeth confirmed that Broomewode was a special place for witches––an energy vortex, she called it. I began to wonder whether maybe my birth mom was a witch, too.

I'd had a vision of her, pregnant and distressed, running away from something, or someone, when I'd been at Broomewode Hall. But this still left me none the wiser about that mysterious painting and whether the lady in it was even alive. I had so many questions and no answers.

So far, my attempts to get inside Broomewode Hall had been thwarted. Its owners, Lord and Lady Frome, were notoriously private. I'd tried to talk to Katie Donegal, the manor house cook, who'd worked for the Champney family for thirty years and knew all the local gossip. But she was weirdly reluctant to tell me anything about my only clue—that I looked like someone named Valerie who'd lived in the village more than twenty years ago. I was certain Katie was holding back, and since it was so busy during filming over the weekend, I decided to arrive a bit earlier than scheduled and come up with an inventive way to get past those intimidating oak doors.

I guessed now was the time to start waking up my dormant witchy powers, whatever they were. I hoped that I could do super-cool stuff, like levitate. Or become invisible! All I knew for certain was that using my powers for personal gain was strictly off the table. So I needed, no, I was champing at the bit to ask the great Elspeth Peach a zillion questions about being a witch. She'd given me a few details, but I was no closer to understanding the full picture. Plus, despite the unfortunate start to the series, my competitive nature hadn't dampened one bit. I wanted to show the judges, Elspeth and Jonathon, that I was a brilliant baker, too. All in all, it's fair to say that instead of getting some R and R and my A-game ready for the second episode of *The Great British Baking Contest*, I was distracted and antsy, counting down the hours till I could load up my car and haul my witchy butt back to the inn.

Instead of waiting until Friday evening, when the

remaining contestants were expected to arrive, I left early Friday morning. I packed and put together some food for Gateau (turned out she had a penchant for organic roast chicken—of course my familiar would be a high-maintenance gourmet) and heaved my suitcase into my car. Gateau liked to ride up front, so I settled her into the passenger seat, and she promptly fell asleep the moment the engine began to rumble.

Fifty minutes later, having miraculously avoided a speeding ticket, I was back.

I let Gateau out, and she scampered happily toward the garden while I fetched my case.

I came around the corner of the building and had to smile as Gateau pounced on the moving shadow of a leaf flickering on the ground. I paused under a blossom tree, breathing deep, enjoying the peace of the day. However, that peace was suddenly shattered by the sound of a man shouting. The gruff voice boomed, "Don't you walk away from me, ye great numpty. I'm telling you it can't be done. It would be murder."

Naturally, at the word murder, my ears perked up.

The speaker had a local Somerset accent, and though I couldn't yet identify him, I was certain I'd heard that voice before. The man who answered him, also sounding as though they were in the middle of an argument, had a posh, smooth accent. "The bees will only be moved a mile. How could that possibly hurt them?"

I heard a thump as though one of the two had punched something, perhaps his opponent, and the Somerset voice cried out with fury, "You can move beehives two feet or you can move them more than three miles, but less than that, they'll go back to the place they remember, fly around looking for that hive until they die. If you move them a mile, you might as well spray them with insecticide and be done with it."

Bees? He was talking about murdering bees?

"Then perhaps that's what I'll do. I don't think you quite understand. I have a deadly allergy to bees. I'm afraid to walk about on my own property."

Yet another cry of helpless rage blasted through the calm of a sleepy Somerset midmorning. "Your property! I like that. My own dad worked his whole life on that farm. And I should have had it after him. Lord Frome promised."

"That's none of my affair," the other man said in a slow, condescending tone, as though this argument had been had many times before. "You must take that up with the current earl. He's the one who rented the farm to me, which he had a legal right to do, and which gives me a legal right to live there. Unharassed."

"Your kind. You make me sick. I won't let you destroy the work of a lifetime. I won't." A man practically exploded around the corner of the pub and stormed past where I was standing, very still, in the shade of the tree. He was so angry, he didn't notice me standing there quietly. Even Gateau froze as the man stomped by in a thundering great temper. I was right. I had heard that voice before. I recognized him as Peter Puddifoot, who was a gardener or groundskeeper for Broomewode Hall.

He kicked gravel as he stomped along, then paused as though undecided before turning into the pub entrance. I decided to follow. If the second man who'd been in that argument came around the corner with less fury, he might catch me eavesdropping. He hadn't appeared yet, so perhaps he'd gone in the other direction. That or he was taking a minute to cool down.

Curious about this bee-murdering business, I dragged my case toward the pub's entrance, hoping Eve would be on duty and in the mood to gossip.

CHAPTER 2

*I*nside the inn, I rushed straight to the bar to see if Eve was working. There were a few people having lunch, and no one that I recognized but Peter Puddifoot, who'd joined a group at a large table. They were probably locals who stayed well away from the film-crew madness that descended at the weekends. He leaned in and was talking in furious undertones. I was pretty sure I could guess the context.

To my delight, Eve's warm, smiling face was behind the bar, and the minute she finished pouring a pint of Somerset cider, she stepped out and enveloped me in a giant hug.

"Poppy, sweetheart, you're early. And you look so well. I can't believe it's been a week since all that tragic business happened. It feels like a bad dream."

I agreed with Eve, and we caught up on the week. Like me, she'd had trouble settling back into a routine. "Everyone who works around Broomewode Hall is on edge, though it had hit the crew hardest. They couldn't believe someone they'd worked so closely alongside, drank pints with in the pub and even invited into their homes was capable of murder."

"And Gordon seemed so nice." I still couldn't get over that the man who'd mic'd me up and flirted so ineptly was a killer.

"It's still the main topic of gossip among the locals," she whispered, pointing at the table of men who were tucking into plates of fish-and-chips and burgers, most enjoying a pint of something along with the food. I felt hungry simply watching them eat.

I wanted to ask Eve about the fight I'd overheard but didn't want the gardener to overhear me. Besides, I had more important things to do. Unpacking would be a good start. It would be nice if I could show up on camera without looking like my clothes were all creased.

Eve fetched a key from one of the hooks that lined the back of the bar and pressed it into my hand. "You've all been given the same rooms as last week. You should feel right at home." And safe, too, I guessed. But it didn't feel weird to be back here, even though last week someone had tried to murder me. Eve was right. It did feel like home.

"You fancy a drink first, Poppy? Tea or coffee? Something a little stronger?"

I was about to refuse (I needed to get going if I was going to get back into Broomewode Hall today) when a guffawing racket exploded from the crowded table and startled me. It was the kind of noise that only British men seemed to be able to make when they gathered in groups. It was loud and kind of obnoxious. Peter Puddifoot was looking pretty pleased with himself, so I guessed he'd cracked the joke that caused the rest of his group to double up with laughter. No doubt the butt of the joke was even now fuming over their argument.

There was another man watching the merriment. He sat alone with a pint of beer in front of him. He had brown hair and a pale complexion and was wearing a cheap-looking suit. He looked like a businessman and, from his dejected expression, not the most successful one.

"I think I'll go up to my room and unpack first," I said to Eve. "I'll come down a bit later for some lunch." I'd become so wrapped up in the overheard argument that I'd nearly forgotten to ask Eve's advice about the first baking challenge tomorrow. "Eve, do you have any idea where I'd find local produce?" We weren't supposed to let anything about the production slip, but it would be pretty obvious to Eve why I was asking.

Her nose wrinkled as she gave my question some thought. "It's a bit early for fruits. Of course, there are root vegetables and apples and things, but you might try the gift shop. We sell local jams and sweets. Might be a start?"

"Of course. Thank you." I'd never been inside the gift shop in an outbuilding beside the inn. I'd assumed it was for the tourists and *Baking Contest* fans who came on tours when they weren't actively filming. However, if they sold local edibles, I'd definitely have a look. I'd brought some apples and pears, both grown in Somerset, and some nuts. I had an idea for an upside-down cake, but I needed to add some pizzazz to it or come up with something else by tomorrow. I thought it was a cruel trick of the show to make us use fresh produce so early in the growing season, but maybe that was the point. To see how innovative we could be.

Eve leaned across the bar and kissed my cheek. "It's good to have you back."

I beamed at Eve and got up to leave, swinging my overstuffed bag across my shoulder. Struggling a bit under its weight, I staggered to the door to fetch Gateau and collided slap-bang into an old, tall, very elegantly dressed man with a sweep of gray hair that was combed away from his high fore-head. He stood back, a horrified expression on his face, and brushed down his navy cashmere sweater and flannel trousers as if I'd left a sticky mark on him. Then I saw that some of Gateau's black fur had somehow transferred from me to him. Now that I was a cat mom, I usually had cat hair on me. "So sorry," I murmured.

The man said, "Excuse me," and then stood aside so that I could pass. I noticed his brown brogues were perfectly polished. Unlike my sneakers, which had mud caked on their sides.

He'd barely walked into the pub when he recoiled at the sight of Peter Puddifoot and his cronies, glared at the man alone at his table, then turned around again, heading straight to the door, his color heightened. He gave me a wide berth as he walked quickly out the door.

I followed him out a, nd watched as he strode over to a dusty old Land Rover in the parking lot. How strange. He'd obviously planned to go inside, perhaps for lunch, and suddenly changed his mind. I hadn't heard him speak more than a mumble, but I suspected this was the man who'd been arguing with the groundskeeper.

I scraped the dried mud off my shoes as best I could. Gateau appeared from beneath a bush and pounced on a swinging shoelace.

I scooped her up, retrieved my bag again, and we climbed the stairs to my room. I opened the door and stopped dead in my tracks. Resting on top of the perfectly made bed, his sneaker-clad feet on the ironed lines of the cozy red blanket, was a man staring up at the ceiling, arms tucked behind his head. He suddenly sat up, and I caught a flash of familiar red hair.

"Gerry! What on earth?" I dropped my bag to the ground with a thud.

"Ah, darlin' Poppy, you're early. What a nice surprise," said my friendly neighborhood ghost, swinging his legs and shuffling to the edge of my bed.

His red hair was as spiky as ever, and his shirt was still patterned with cars and trucks. If it weren't for the shadowy line around his body, I would have thought last week had been a nightmare and Gerry was in my room to talk strategy for this week's show. However, he'd been sent home from the show and pushed off this mortal coil all on the same day. I suspected he was having trouble adjusting.

"I can't tell you how much I've missed you this week. I've been bored out of my mind."

"I don't understand. You haven't moved on?"

"Move on where? I can move between this pub and the tent. That's it. And there's absolutely nothing to do here. No one to banter with, no one to flirt with... I went all poltergeist on the honeymoon couple in the big room upstairs, that was fun, but I may have overdone it because they checked out early."

I tried not to laugh; it would only encourage him. "Oh, Gerry. That's not very nice. Being cheeky in the afterlife is not like being cheeky...well, in this life. You need to be compassionate. Don't go around giving ghosts a bad name."

He gave me a salute. "Okay, ma'am," he said. "I'll do better."

I liked Gerry, and I felt sorry for him, but I'd really hoped he'd be gone when I arrived. As in dearly departed gone. All the way gone.

He stood and stretched. "But seeing you has cheered me up to no end. And I've got a ringside seat to the baking competition this week."

I shook my finger at him like I was a schoolteacher and he was a naughty boy. He'd caused enough mischief on the set already. "Do not start interfering," I told him. "You have to promise me."

He pouted. "But I could help you win. I can't move things. Yet. But if I stand right in someone's face and glare at them, even though they can't see me, it definitely throws them off stride."

"I bet. But I don't want you to do that."

"Well, if you change your mind, I'll fix it so you win."

I shook my head again. "No, Gerry. I don't want to win anything that's been 'fixed.' And thanks for your vote of confidence in me."

He grinned. "You're a good baker, Pops. But you've got some competition to beat. Maggie is a clear front-runner, and the gorgeous Florence is right behind her. I think Gaurav could surprise us all. And Hamish is watching and waiting for his chance to impress. Mark my words."

I suspected he was right, but he'd all but said I was in the bottom of the pack. Great.

"But hey, check out what I've spent my week perfecting." He jumped on the bed, levitating so high his head disappeared through the ceiling. I gave him a quick round of applause, but I'd seen that trick countless times with other ghost pals. I decided not to burst his bubble. What else could a ghost in limbo do to pass the time?

When he came back down, he said, "Guess what?"

"What?" I unzipped my case and started unpacking.

"Marcus Hoare will *not* be joining you this week. I overheard the producers talking in the pub. Well, I joined their table, not that they noticed. Turns out sabotaging another contestant, i.e., me, did not endear Marcus to the judges or the producers of this fine show. He claims he had to go to New York for a work emergency for several weeks." Gerry tapped the side of his nose. "Sounds like a convenient excuse to me."

"I don't know, Gerry. It could be true. Marcus was seriously competitive about his baking. I'd be surprised if he gave up so easily."

Gerry humphed in response. Suddenly, he was behind me, watching me hang shirts and blouses in the antique oak wardrobe.

"Looks like someone couldn't decide what to wear this week."

"I know. It's so hard packing. Will it be hot in the tent? Cool? In between? I've tried to prepare for every kind of weather. It was much chillier last week than I'd expected. I don't want to get caught out again."

"I like the striped shirt. It'll look great on telly."

"Thanks for the fashion advice." To be honest, I really didn't need advice about what to wear from someone who wore shirts patterned with cars and trucks. In fact, I'd planned to consult Gina, who was the hair and makeup expert, when she arrived on set. But since Gerry was already dead, I didn't want to hurt his feelings or make him suffer any more than he had already. I finished hanging my clothes and turned back. He was staring at Gateau, who was staring right back at him. "I don't care much for cats," he said.

Yes. I could use this to my advantage.

"Well, since you went and disappeared on me, she's my new best friend here. You'll have to get used to her."

"Can she see me?" They looked like they were having a staring contest.

"I have no idea. Maybe."

"If you can see me, little cat, then vamoose." He made shooing motions with his hands. Gateau didn't change her expression or move so much as a cat hair. I couldn't tell whether she couldn't see him or was simply ignoring the annoying ghost.

Now that I'd unpacked, I wanted to get over to Broome-wode Hall. I didn't think Gerry could go that far, but in case, I told a little white lie. "Gateau and I are pretty wiped from the drive this morning, so we're going to take a short catnap. There are a few locals in the pub downstairs, if you fancy messing with them."

Gerry sighed. "Borrrrring. But who am I to stand—I mean float—in the way of you and your beauty sleep, Pops. You're going to need it if you want to wow on national television this weekend and capture the hearts of the masses." He made a motion as though presenting me with a bouquet of invisible flowers. "Adieu," he said, and disappeared through the door.

Phew, that was easier than I thought. Now if only getting into Broomewode Hall would be that easy, I'd be a happy little witch.

CHAPTER 3

*S*ince I felt pressed for time if I was going to find a way into Broomewode Hall, do my snooping and still be back in time to hit the market for some local ingredients for the first baking challenge tomorrow, I didn't have time to stop for a yummy pub lunch, much as I wanted to. I contented myself with a packet of crisps from behind the bar and one of the green apples they kept in a bowl in the front hall for guests.

Although Gerry had made fun of me, when I stepped back outside, I was grateful to my panicked self who had overpacked. Even though it was only late April, the afternoon sun was bright. I felt my cheeks flush with warmth and slipped out of my pale blue cardigan, which Gina fondly referred to as my granny cardi, and put it into my tote bag.

The gift shop was open. I might as well give it a try. I told Gateau to wait outside and went into the pretty little cottage that was jammed with things to entice shoppers. Naturally, right up front was a display related to *The Great British Baking Contest*. Cookbooks by Elspeth and Jonathon, most of them signed by the celebrity bakers, were stacked beside smaller offerings of cookbooks put out by some of the more successful contestants who'd come before me.

There were tea towels and baking tins, coffee mugs and T-shirts and exact copies of the aprons we wore on the show. As I walked deeper into the shop, a kindly-looking older woman looked up over her glasses from where she was dusting a shelf of knickknacks. "Hello. Can I help you with anything?"

I didn't want to tell her I was shopping for the baking challenge tomorrow, so I said I was just browsing. And it was kind of fun to poke around. Once past the *baking contest* wares, I encountered a lot of items promoting Broomewode Hall. Tapestry cushions featuring the manor house, cushions with the British flag, pheasants, and one of tulips that I'd have bought for my living room if it wasn't so expensive.

Oh, and what about those fireplace tools? My little cottage featured a huge fireplace and hearth in the kitchen. I thought it would be fun to display something made of black iron, and these were clearly hand-forged. I went closer. There were fire pokers, full sets of tools, ornate hooks for hanging planter baskets, I supposed, or maybe bird feeders. When I looked at the cards attached, they informed me that these items were indeed hand-forged at a place called Broomewode Smithy. The card also informed me that I couldn't afford them, either. Not unless I spent less time practicing my baking and more time on my freelance graphic design.

"They're lovely, aren't they?" the saleswoman said, coming closer. "And made right here in the village."

"Really? Yes, they're lovely."

"The man who makes them took over the old blacksmith's shop right here in Broomewode Village. I believe he was a podiatrist, but when he retired here, he took up the old craft. He's very good, isn't he?"

"Yes." I didn't want to tell this nice woman that I was too poor for the former podiatrist's wares, so I moved on, until I came to the food section.

She told me to let her know if I needed help with anything and went back to her work. Good. I wanted to peruse the foods in my own time. There were plenty of Somerset apple products, of course. Applesauce, fancy bottles of the local cider, dried apples. There were jams and jellies, everything from brambleberry to quince. There was toffee and wrapped chocolate bars bearing the photograph of Broomewode Hall. Nothing magically jumped out at me, but I bought a jar of the quince jelly. I might be able to use that in my glaze.

I tucked the jar into my tote bag after paying for it, and my faithful kitten and I set out again.

Gateau was trotting by my side, but she was looking up at me as if to say, *So what now? What's the plan?* The problem was, despite thinking about it every spare minute I wasn't practicing cake-baking, I hadn't come up with any plausible ways to get inside the Hall *and* into the dining room to examine the painting up close. Among my brilliant ideas had been, learning to climb drainpipes, scaling the roof, and dropping into the Hall through the skylight. Obviously, I scratched that idea. I was fairly certain Broomewode Hall didn't boast skylights.

I couldn't afford to get caught snooping again. Benedict Champney, the slightly mysterious son, had already warned me away twice, and now both the Earl and Lady Frome knew my face, and neither had been particularly nice to it.

I decided there was nothing for it but to sneak onto the property, try the servants' entrance and hope that Katie answered the door. I could ask about her broken arm and try to get her reminiscing about the old days and a woman named Valerie.

Somehow, I'd find a way to get into that dining room and study the painting. I continued my walk to the manor house, trying to root around in my mind for something that could pass as a spell of invisibility, when Gateau began to hiss.

"What's the matter, little thing?" I asked, looking down. I saw the problem immediately. A friendly-looking dog was bounding toward us. It was black and white and rangy. I was no expert on breeds, but it looked like a border collie heading straight toward us. I guessed even magical cats weren't immune to the age-old cat and dog rivalry. The dog was a beauty though, sleek with black and white fur and an inquisitive face. He seemed to have taken a shine to my Gateau, whose hissing was having absolutely no effect whatsoever. He came closer and tried to nudge her nose with his, but this move sent her running. Straight up a tree.

"Oh, Gateau," I said, staring up at her forlorn face buried in the branches. "The dog was only being friendly."

She mewed in response, and scrambled up another branch.

"Come on," I coaxed. "He isn't going to stick around. You climb down. We've got important business to attend to, you and I." I stopped, aware that if anyone walked past, I would sound like a total loony.

But, in fact, the dog didn't seem to be going anywhere. He'd dashed off for a quick lap of Gateau's tree of solace, and now reappeared with an orange ball, which he dropped at my feet. I laughed and picked up the ball and threw it obligingly. He really was adorable. As he bounded away to fetch the ball, I looked around the grounds for his owner, but there was no one in sight. Was he a stray? Surely not with that glossy coat and his own ball.

"You must belong to someone," I mused as he returned with the ball, panting and lowering himself on his haunches, front paws out, waiting expectantly at my feet, eyes traveling between the dirt-speckled, saliva-covered ball and my face. I had a feeling I was going to tire of this game long before he did.

Gateau hissed again from above, but this time, I think it was aimed at me. "I know. I never should have thrown the ball."

I BENT down to stroke the collie's lovely black and white fur and found a red collar. I swiveled it around and found a tag that read Broomewode Farm and a phone number. Aha. Oh, dearest wandering dog, you may have bought me another chance to get closer to the Champneys. Surely returning a mischievous working dog was the perfect excuse to be on their property...and perhaps do a little snooping. Now, all I had to do was convince Gateau to come down from her hiding place.

But it seemed luck was on my side today, or maybe it was something more than that, as Gateau was already making her own way down. Not elegantly. It was more of a bum shuffle with some sorrowful mewling than a graceful descent.

Gateau, finally, made it to the bottom of the tree and then

looked up at me like I'd presented her with a whole roast chicken but taken it away from her again before she'd had a bite. I bent down, picked her up and rubbed the top of her head.

And there was that orange ball again. I threw it along the path in front of us and watched the collie bound after it, his bushy tail wagging. In the distance, he picked up the ball but carried on walking. He turned his head to check that we were following. I smiled. He obviously had a strong herding instinct, and he was herding me exactly where I wanted to go.

I guessed the three of us made for an unlikely crew, but as we walked I felt a sense of peace and purpose. The sun on the back of my neck felt like a warm embrace. The silvery-green leaves of the whitebeam trees shone. The sky was a cerulean blue—a description I'd learned through experimenting with food coloring. I walked with a long stride, cradling Gateau. We passed an ornamental lake sparkling in the sun. I wanted to linger and take a moment to stare into its depths, hoping for another image of the woman I thought was my mother to appear across its peaceful surface, but the collie had other ideas, and ran back to make sure we were following. He was excited by something. But to my dismay, the collie didn't lead us to Broomewode Hall. Instead, he turned left, away from Broomewode Hall, down a path I'd never noticed before.

Rather than the polished and freakishly smooth gravel of the grounds' main path, I now trod on chunky wood chips. Brambles intertwined with sprawling green bushes. A gentle breeze stirred in the horse chestnut trees to my left. The collie bounded on, every few moments stopping to turn and check I was still following. I wanted to tell him, *Duh, of course I'm following you. Take me to your master so I can do some detective work.*

With her nemesis safely in the distance, Gateau leapt out of my arms, shook herself down and began to trot alongside me with a straight back and her little nose in the air. I guessed she was trying to recover her dignity.

Soon I saw why the collie had sped up: In the distance, an outline of what looked like a farm emerged from among what must have been about two hundred acres of rolling green hills. The collie broke into a run now, heading toward a huge barn, its curved roof catching the light. The path narrowed and changed from wood chips to stone, and either side was planted with laurel hedging and bright springy fern. Up ahead, beside the barn, stood a large farmhouse, crafted from the golden Somerset stone. The surrounding garden was in full bloom with a sloping rockery, and I couldn't help but notice that its herb patch was absolutely bursting with fragrant green offerings. It put my own rambling herb garden to shame. Next to the farmhouse was an annex, where the farmhands must have stayed during harvesting seasons when the farming industry round here was booming. I couldn't tell what it was they farmed here, though. The dog began barking, and then a wide door painted a fawn-gray opened.

"Sly? There you are," a commanding female voice called out.

A woman emerged from the doorway. She was tall, with a high forehead and a determined jaw. Her deep red hair was graying at the sides and cropped short, though it curled a little at the edges, giving her a girlish look. She was wearing gumboots and a worn, dark green jacket that had a few specks of mud clinging to its sleeves. The dog rushed over to her, and she gave him a hearty pat before admonishing him for running off. She straightened and saw me hovering.

"He's well named," she said, gesturing to the dog. "He's a sly one, that's for sure. Plays to the sound of his own fiddle."

I laughed. "I'd like to say I found him and brought him back, but it was more like he found me and herded me along."

"Well, thank you, either way," she said, smiling wide so that her eyes crinkled. "Aha!" She pointed at the orange ball in my hand. "That blasted ball. We lost it walking the other day, and he wouldn't settle without it."

"He found it all by himself," I admitted. "I was just the chump who threw it for him as many times as he wanted." Sly stood between us, his mouth open, showing his teeth. I swear he was laughing at me.

The woman caught sight of my kitten and walked forward to greet Gateau. "I see you don't travel alone."

Gateau mewed in response.

"She's a special kind of cat..." I stopped. How could I explain that Gateau, despite freaking out at one, behaved more like a faithful dog than a cat? "She follows me around— a bit like a furry guardian angel."

As if on cue, Sly ran up to Gateau, panting and wagging his bushy tail. She hissed in response, and disappeared behind my ankles.

"Adorable." The woman put her hand out. "Susan Bentley. Welcome to Broomewode Farm."

I introduced myself and Gateau, and explained that I was one of the bakers, here before filming to settle in.

"Well, of course, I could have guessed that," Susan said. "We're only a small community. And we don't get many bright young things around here. They all move to Bath or London the minute they're old enough." She smiled wryly. "Then retire back down here. Will you come in for tea? And meet my husband, Arnold."

My thoughts had stayed on the words *We're only a small community*. Susan might not be one of the Champneys, but she *was* their neighbor. And since she already gave the impression that everybody knew everybody here, maybe she could help me understand more about who Valerie might have been and why the Champneys were so eager to keep me off their property. I was about to accept the tea invitation when the sound of squawking birds came to my ears. I was startled. They sounded panicked, and I immediately thought of foxes and henhouses.

"Oh, Sly," Susan Bentley said, sounding exasperated. "He will herd the chickens."

She rushed around the side of the barn, and I followed. Behind the barn was a large enclosure where ten or twelve hens had obviously been happily foraging before the mad herder decided to follow his instincts. Now they were crying out their alarm and running about.

"He won't do them any harm," Susan assured me. "I often put the newly-hatched chicks next to him at night to keep warm. He's that gentle."

To my amazement, the chickens, in spite of their cries of outrage and flapping wings, were heading into a wire-fenced enclosure that contained a large and new-looking coop. Sly was in his element, racing in circles that grew tighter as he nudged the chickens toward the open gate.

In a big field behind the coop, I could just make out four

beehives. This seemed like a real working farm but on a small scale.

Susan shook her head. "I usually leave them out a bit longer, but he's put them away so nicely now, I'll leave them and let them out again later." As the last chicken strutted into the pen, Sly backed away and turned to make sure I was watching. I had the strangest idea he was showing off for me. Or maybe for Gateau, who was washing a paw, completely uninterested in the herding of fowl. Susan closed and latched the gate, and the chickens seemed perfectly content pecking at their food or walking around as though making sure their home was as they'd left it.

As we walked back to the farmhouse, I had to pick my way through some muddy patches. I'd packed a dozen cardigans but no gumboots. Go figure.

Sly had left his orange ball back by the house, and was walking at a steady pace, with his bushy tail wagging happily from side to side like a pendulum.

"How long have you had the farm?" I asked, hoping she'd say thirty years or more. I longed to find someone, anyone, who might have known the woman named Valerie. Susan Bentley looked to be around late fifties or early sixties, so she could well have known the young woman who'd lived in the area twenty-six or more years ago.

"About four years," Susan said, bursting my bubble.

"Only four years?" I replied, hearing how disappointed I sounded.

"Yes. We lived in London. We came down here when my husband retired."

"I see. It looks like a very active retirement." I was mostly wondering how to steer the conversation around to Broomewode Hall. *And* avoid sinking my sneakers into muddy pockets as we crossed the long, green grass.

Susan pointed at the green hills, where sheep were grazing and several little lambs were playfully scampering around. It was an idyllic scene. "Sly really wants to herd the sheep, of course, and they do let him help from time to time, but he's more of a pet than a working dog."

I wasn't sure Sly had got that memo.

"You must try my fruitcake," she said. It was amazing how people did that. From the moment I got the call that I was one of the contestants, I found that the second I mentioned I'd be on *The Great British Baking Contest,* everyone had a special cake, pie or loaf they wanted me to taste. "The recipe's been handed down through my family for generations. Really, I think the secret is the amount of brandy."

I chuckled, as she'd intended me to. Cake and cooks were close enough, so I moved the conversation toward something I was much more interested in than fruitcake. "I met Katie Donegal, the cook at the manor house, last week. Do you know her?"

"Oh yes, of course I know Katie. She's worked for the Champneys for years. She broke her arm, poor thing. She really ought to be more careful at her age. I don't get to chat to her much, we're both so busy, but I do let her pick gooseberries from our land to make gooseberry jam. She'd have picked the first crop by now if she didn't have a broken arm. They grow along the wall of the old chapel tower, where they get lots of sun but are protected from the elements. We get gooseberries weeks earlier than everybody else," she informed me with pride.

In spite of my wish to learn more about Katie and my

past, I was also a contestant in a baking show, and our first challenge was to bake a cake cooked with local produce. And here I'd discovered gooseberries ripe weeks earlier than everywhere else?

I could have kissed Sly for bringing me here, slobbery ball and all. "So it's like a microclimate?"

"Yes, exactly. And this year, the crop is well ahead of season. They're ready to pick."

I glanced around looking for a tower and saw it on a hill, behind a stand of trees. It was built of local stone and looked weathered and romantic. "There was an abbey here once with a thriving nunnery. Of course, it was all destroyed in Henry VIII's time, but the tower remains."

"It's so picturesque."

"I agree. I wish I could paint so I could capture it in different lights and seasons."

I hoped I could use some of Susan's produce for tomorrow's challenge. We knew in advance that the first challenge was going to be to use British produce in a cake. Originally my plan had been to handpick the new crop of strawberries that grew on a farm not too far from Broomewode Hall. But after talking it through with Gina, I realized that would probably be everyone else's plan, too. At least the strawberry bit. So I needed something that would make me stand out, show that I had some flair and imagination. If I could get Susan to agree to let me at her crop, they'd be so much fresher, not to mention more local, than anything I'd be able to find in the village grocers.

"Susan, I know this might be a cheeky question, but could I make a gooseberry upside-down cake for my challenge this week? It would be so wonderful if you could spare some of your fruit. I'm sure they're absolutely delicious, and I could explain how I'd picked them myself from your land when the cameras were on me. It would be a great talking point. Plus, it might be good for business? Millions of viewers would know about whatever you produce here."

I stopped and gulped. I was so not getting used to the idea that soon millions of people would know my name and my baking abilities. Or not, as might be the case.

"What a wonderful idea, Poppy," Susan said, smiling. "We sell our local honey and jams in small batches, but there's room to grow. You could make us famous. Besides, I know some great facts about gooseberries that you could slip in." She told me that the gooseberries have grown in Britain since the time of Henry VIII, when they were transported from India on boats. The fruit, as well as being delicious, was also used as a medicine to treat fevers, and in the sixteenth century they were recommended to plague victims. Poor guys. As if the humble gooseberry was going to do *them* any good. Gooseberries had been used in many Ayurvedic and Unani medicines.

Phew. I was going to have to write all that down. All that info would make a great talking point if I managed to get one of the hosts to ask the right questions.

"Tell you what," Susan carried on, "I'll throw in some fresh farm eggs too, from our chickens. In spite of being herded by Sly, the chickens are so happy here, roaming outside, eating healthy organic food, that the eggs taste much better than anything you'd get in the supermarkets. The yolks are creamy and a delightful orange color."

I thanked her profusely, but she just smiled and shook her head. "I've also got a new batch of honey from our bees.

Would that be of any use? Not to brag, but our bees are pretty superior too. They are spoiled for choice round here, what with our lavender bushes. Plus they can feast on the elderflower, roses—not to mention our fruit trees. You have to try the honey. It's rich and mellow."

"That would amazing. And so generous of you. This competition is so tough. If a happy hen or contented bee can give me the upper hand, then I'll take it."

"It's a pleasure. We sell our products mostly through gift shops and farmers' markets. It's mainly a hobby, at the moment, but it helps pay the bills."

"You seem like you've always farmed."

She gave a short laugh and shook her head. "Arnold, my husband, was the one who wanted this farm. We moved here from London after his health began to deteriorate from sixteen-hour days working in the city. They work you to the bone in those ghastly places. It wasn't until we moved here and he got stung that he discovered he was allergic. He has an EpiPen, of course. But after a few too many close calls, he's cautious. Perhaps overly cautious, but I do sympathize." She sighed. "Still, it's meant more work for me."

Susan blushed and stopped talking. No matter how long I'd spent living in England, I couldn't get used to how proper the British were. They seemed to be embarrassed by the sharing of any small personal detail. I gently smiled at her in a way that I hoped said *Look, don't worry, we all over-share* without actually having to say it. Maybe she didn't get to talk to that many people during the day, what with all her farm chores.

Susan seemed to gather herself and ran a hand through her red hair. "Let me fetch you the eggs and honey. Meanwhile, you can go pick as many gooseberries as you need—just leave a few for Katie so that she can make jam—if the poor thing can, with one arm out of action."

Ding ding ding! For the second time that day, I could've thrown my arms around Susan. Without knowing it, she'd given me the perfect excuse to go back to Broomewode Hall. I told her I'd pick some extra gooseberries for Katie and deliver them myself. She seemed delighted with the idea. I felt like Susan was my new guardian angel.

She even gave me two straw baskets to collect the berries in. One for me and one for Katie.

Talk about a productive outing. I now had fresh local fruit for my challenge tomorrow and the perfect excuse to visit Broomewode Hall.

Things were definitely looking up.

CHAPTER 4

ollowing Susan's directions, Gateau and I continued our extended walking tour of the farm. I could see why the Bentleys had chosen this place to escape from the fast-paced chaos of London life. Surrounding us were majestic oak trees, their trunks gnarled by time, and tall, willowy ash trees, delicately covered with creeping vines. Orchards of fruit trees and vines and in the distance the sheep, like so many clouds in a green sky.

If the events of last weekend weren't still so fresh in my mind, this place would be totally idyllic. The sun warmed my back, and there was a gentle breeze that cooled my cheeks as I braced the uphill climb. Even still, I felt sweat gather at the base of my neck. I'd spent too much time testing cake recipes recently and too little on the treadmill.

The old tower was made of the same golden stone as the farm and manor but had obviously been beaten up by time and weather. Parts were crumbling and streaked with dirt. Patches of green showed where plants had taken hold in the most unlikely places. Maybe this had been part of a nunnery, but I felt that there was also something romantic about it. I imagined it was where lovers had met in secret, maybe if their families didn't agree on the match or if they wanted to steal a kiss and fumble. Gateau sprinted ahead. I realized she was chasing a butterfly. My heart melted; she might be my familiar, but she was still a playful kitty.

I followed Gateau and found the crop of gooseberries at the base of the tower. Through some lucky chance, a few low stone walls had survived on this warm, south side of the tower. The trees blocked any harsh winds, and the stone trapped heat. No wonder the gooseberries were miles ahead of the rest of their kind. I bet you could grow melons and grapes in here.

The crop was more plentiful than I could have hoped. I'd never had the pleasure of foraging gooseberries myself before, and I was surprised at how beautiful the plants were. The oval fruits were a vivid green, patterned with thin white lines and nestled among bundles of small palm-shaped leaves. I put my tote bag on top of a solid bit of wall and began to pick the berries. They were perfectly ripe, firm to the touch. I could tell they'd be juicy and perfect for my cake. And for Katie, too. I would be a jam heroine.

It was soothing work. The odd bee buzzed by, and birds sang. The sunshine felt pleasantly warm, and my mind drifted to tomorrow as I pictured my cake turning out brilliantly.

I put one full basket on the wall beside my tote and started filling the second. I probably had enough, but it wouldn't hurt to have extras in case I made any silly mistakes on baking day. I didn't want to end up scorching my syrup and not being able to make it a second time.

Not that I was planning to scorch my syrup. Where did that even come from?

I went back to picking fruit, focusing on the slightly green and spicy scent, their sun-warm plumpness as I chose the ripest berries.

Almost in the distance I heard a vague rumbling sound, but it barely registered. And then I heard a dog barking. It sounded hysterical and very close. I glanced up to find Sly racing toward me, head down in herding mode. I looked around in surprise. Had the chickens escaped? And then he was on me, head butting my legs, nipping at my heels.

I JUMPED IN SHOCK. "Ow." Did he think I was one of his sheep? He barked, and before he could nip me again, I ran, him chasing me with determination until I turned around and faced him. "Sly! What are you—" I was interrupted by a crash. A huge slab of stone had fallen from the top of the tower. As stone hit stone, small pebbles bounced. It landed exactly where I'd been standing. Half the bush was smashed, and the edge of a wicker handle was all I could see of the second basket I'd been filling.

Sly began to bark at the fallen stone, running toward it and back again as though giving it a piece of his mind.

As for me, I sank down to the ground, my back against the wall, and stared. I didn't want to be overdramatic, but I was certain that if Sly hadn't herded me away, I'd have suffered the same fate as that basket.

Sly came over to where I sat, too stunned to move, and nudged me with his nose. I patted him, noticing my hands were shaking. We both stared at the flattened gooseberries. "Well, that's one way to make jam," I said. And not my preferred method.

My heart was beating so fast, I thought it was going to burst out of my chest. Where the heck were my witchy powers when I needed them most? Like when a giant slab of stone was about to crush me?

Sly leaned into me as I stroked his lovely long nose, and then Gateau walked daintily along the top of the wall until she reached me, then jumped down and settled on my other side. I stroked them both, happily sandwiched between my animal guardians.

But Sly didn't stick around for any more compliments. He put his head to one side, and the ruff on his neck rose. With a low growl, he ran around the side of the tower and began barking again. Gateau climbed onto my lap and began licking my hands like she was trying to lick my wounds away. The dog, however, kept barking. "All right, all right," I muttered, slowly getting to my feet. "I'm coming. Don't bark the rest of the building down."

I followed the sound around the base of the tower and found Sly on the other side, sniffing at what looked to be the entrance. I peered into the dark and saw the beginning of a spiral stone staircase. Sly stopped sniffing and started barking again. I heard shouting. I turned and saw Susan running up the hill toward me. "Don't go in there. It's not safe."

A spurt of laughter escaped me, another symptom of shock, as there was nothing funny about a near miss with death. "Neither is picking gooseberries," I replied and led her around to where the stone had fallen.

"Oh, my goodness, Poppy!" she exclaimed, staring at me and then at the huge slab on the ground, and then looking up at the tower. "I heard the noise but didn't know what it was. Are you all right?"

"I'm not hurt. Only shocked. But I'd be dead if it wasn't for Sly. He literally herded me away from the tower. The stone missed both of us by inches."

The color drained from Susan's face, making her red hair seem even redder. She looked horrified. It was something like the expression I'm sure I made the first time I realized I was seeing a ghost.

She was staring at the handle of her crushed basket. Somehow, it felt more deadly to see a basket associated with produce or picnics crushed like that. "You could have been killed. I feel so responsible. I'm the one who sent you up here. But I'd no idea that the tower was in such a state of disrepair. I haven't been here myself in ages. I knew it was old and damp, but certainly not crumbling."

"You weren't to know," I said, but I was still shaking from the shock.

"It's not the first thing to go wrong on this property. My husband and I settled on Broomewode Farm as our new home only because Arnold and Lord Frome knew each other through work, but I'd no idea how much upkeep an old farm involves. Things go wrong more often than one would hope. Life was so much easier in London. I wonder if I'll ever get used to it here."

I didn't know what to say. The world the Bentleys and Champneys appeared to inhabit was beyond my imagination. I wouldn't mind a farm and acres of land, even if it was a bit downtrodden. When I bought the Olde Bakery, it certainly didn't look like Buckingham Palace. I'd spent months reno-vating the place, pulling up some of the old carpet and replacing it with the same flagstones in the rest of the cottage that I'd found on eBay. I retiled the kitchen and bathroom myself and gave the whole thing a makeover with fancy paint I'd saved and saved for. I guessed the Bentleys were used to living in a flashy London pad. Probably a penthouse. Even still, I *did* know something about feeling displaced, so despite just having had a near-death experience, I smiled at Susan and tried to comfort her.

"Don't worry," I said. "There's no harm done. And Sly is a hero." I looked again at that ominous slab that, now I stared at it, resembled the top of a coffin. "You should put up some rope or something, though, and a sign warning people to keep clear."

She smiled weakly back at me. "Good idea. I'll get someone to do that today. In the meantime, come back to the house and we'll have a cup of tea."

I wasn't so sure that I was in the mood for tea—a stiff vodka tonic would have done the trick—but I picked up the full basket of berries and my bag and followed Susan and Sly back to the farmhouse. Gateau brought up the rear.

The fawn-gray front door was open, and in the entrance a tall man was silhouetted. He was holding a copy of *The Finan-cial Times*, and as we approached, he raised it to shield his eyes from the sun.

"Susan?" he called out. "Is everything all right? I heard something."

"There's been an accident, Arnold, but no one is hurt," she called back.

As we grew closer, I took in his cashmere sweater and

flannels. It was the man I'd almost collided with at the pub, the one I was certain had argued with Peter Puddifoot. Now, in place of his smart brown brogues was a pair of tartan slippers, and reading glasses were hanging around his neck on a silver chain. I said hello and smiled, but if he recognized me, he didn't show it. Not even a blink.

Susan introduced us, and he shook my hand with a palm-crushing grip. She explained about me returning Sly, how I was "one of those charming bakers" and about the gooseberry-picking for my cake. While she was talking, he stared quizzically at Gateau, who had one leg cocked in the air and was giving herself a good clean. So not ladylike.

"We should put up warning signs, Arnold. Not that anyone goes near it except us and Katie Donegal sometimes. Still, I wouldn't want anyone to get hurt."

"I'd come over to the tower to take a look, but I'm afraid you may have stirred up the bees."

Susan looked alarmed. "Oh, I didn't mean you. I'll have Peter Puddifoot or one of the lads do it. Have you got your EpiPen on you, darling?" My ears perked up when she mentioned Peter Puddifoot. He was the man who'd been shouting at her husband not so long ago.

"Of course, I do," he replied, with the air of a man used to repeating himself. He pulled the EpiPen from his pocket. "Never go anywhere without it," he said, turning it over in his large hands. "And luck getting that lazy, no-good Puddifoot to fix anything around this place. He was getting drunk in the pub last time I saw him."

"Well, I'll get someone else, then," she said in a soothing tone.

Peter Puddifoot had indeed been drinking a cider with his

mates in the pub, but he'd been far from getting drunk. There was definitely serious animosity between those two.

"Poppy, are you ready for that tea?"

I was not. Still shocked from almost being obliterated by a slab of falling tower, I didn't want to make small talk with strangers. Besides, if I was gone, they could get busy posting warning signs around that tower. I made my excuses to Susan, explaining that I needed to get ready for tomorrow's challenge.

"I understand," Susan said. "But you must return another time so that I can serve you some of my fruitcake. I'd love your opinion as an expert baker."

She handed me a bag filled with fresh eggs and a glass jar of golden honey. I thanked her and gently placed the bundle in my tote bag. I gave Sly a big old stroke and thanked him for saving me. He wagged his tail in response. He really was a special dog. Arnold gave me the briefest bow of his head and headed back inside with his wife.

The door slammed behind them, and I jumped with a start. My nerves were jangled. If Broomewode was supposed to be a magical place that drew witches to it, why was I continually being confronted by my own mortality? I tapped the amethyst on the necklace around my neck with my nail. "Hello, hello, is this thing on?"

I walked back down the path, my gaze drawn to that ruined tower. It didn't look any different. Just as lonely and romantic as before, only this time, the very sight of it filled me with dread.

Turning resolutely away, I said to my little sidekick, "Shall we go back to the pub and get some lunch or take these gooseberries to Katie?" I wasn't even scheming to get inside; I simply wanted to warn the woman. What if she chose today, of all days, to pick berries? She seemed determined enough to pick one-handed. Or talk one of the kitchen helpers into it. Either way, I wanted to warn the kitchen staff to stay clear.

The sound of an air rifle cracked across the sky. I jumped again, this time nearly dropping my bag of baking goodies. Was Lord Frome shooting clay pigeons again? I was in no fit state to charm my way inside that fortress or tell them that I'd nearly been crushed by their dodgy old tower. A better idea would be to drop off my produce for the weekend's challenge at the tent—while I still had it.

I slung the tote higher up my shoulder and turned in the direction of the tent. Gateau bounded ahead of me and disappeared into the depths of a huge flowering bush. Rather than calling her back, I figured she might need a little *I'm just a cat* time. She'd find me when she needed me or, as was more likely, when I needed her. She might have a bit of an attitude, but that cat certainly knew how to do her job.

A flock of gray birds rushed over my head, their wings beating so rapidly they made a whooshing sound that startled me. I definitely wasn't feeling myself. All week I'd been itching to get back here, and now that I was, I couldn't shake the feeling that something was wrong. Dreadfully wrong.

Was I overreacting about a bit of old stone falling so close to me? Was it witchy intuition, or was I just losing my nerve? I touched the purple stone again and wished with all my might that Elspeth would show up and tell me that everything was all right.

There was a rustle from behind a buckthorn bush, and I wondered what new horror was in store. Wild boars? As I backed away, Benedict Champney emerged. He looked as

surprised to see me as I was to see him. *Way to go, Poppy.*
That's twice in one day you've collided with a strange man.
What else would you like to walk straight into? A door?

"Poppy!" Benedict spluttered. He was wearing an old
flannel shirt with grass stains on it and heavy work trousers
with frayed hems. His hands were encased in big brown work
gloves, and a length of rope was slung over his shoulder. He
had a toolbelt on. This guy. He never wore the same kind of
outfit twice. First some kind of historical getup, then a posh
cashmere sweater, and now he looked more like a gardener.

He paused and studied my face more intently. "You look
awfully pale. Are you all right?"

I wondered if all this equipment was so he could put up
barriers around the tower. I certainly hoped so. "Are you
headed to the tower?"

He looked at me strangely. "What tower?"

Maybe he wasn't heading toward Broomewode Farm at
Susan's behest. Briefly, I explained that Susan Bentley had let
me pick gooseberries at the base of the old tower and that
part of it had fallen and nearly crushed me to death. I found
that even in the short time since it had happened, the incident was taking on a fairy-tale quality. Like it hadn't really
happened or as if it were in the past.

"Good Lord," he said, shaking his head with the same
look of horror as Susan had given me. "You do mean the old
chapel tower?"

How many towers were there around here that tossed
rocks at unsuspecting gooseberry pickers? "Yes. The old
chapel tower at Broomewode Farm."

We both turned to look in the direction of the tower,
though it was invisible from here.

"I thought that's where you were going," I said, gesturing to the rope.

"I've been out mending the fences this morning. It's an endless job." He shifted the rope on his shoulder. "Now I'll have to abandon it and see what I can do about securing the tower."

I nodded, for the second time that day clueless as to how to respond to the woes of the wealthy.

"I'll head over to the farm now. If it's unsafe, we'll have to repair it. There's no tearing down of Grade II listed buildings."

I nodded again, still mute, still having trouble working up a whole lot of pity for these people who owned so much, including a piece of history that they'd no doubt knock down if they could.

Benedict looked concerned again. "Perhaps you'd best have a lie-down? Have you eaten any lunch?"

I shook my head. No wonder I was feeling strange. I was hungry. I guess not even a close call with the grim reaper himself could disrupt my appetite.

I told him I was just going to drop off my foraged ingredients at the tent and then I'd get myself some lunch back at the pub. I felt a bit dizzy and hoped I wouldn't make an utter fool of myself by fainting.

"Shall I walk you to the village? You really look most odd."

And wasn't that what every girl wanted to hear? "No. I'll be fine. I haven't eaten much today, and the shock..."

I waved Benedict goodbye and headed toward the tent. Since I didn't hear rustling leaves and branches snapping behind me, I was fairly certain he was watching me. No doubt making sure I didn't suffer a fatality before getting off his land.

At last I left the path and began to cross the fields toward the tent. From the outside, it looked the same as ever: white and vast, billowing in the breeze. Not even the vaguest suggestion of the terrible events that had happened here last week. I shuddered. I didn't know whether it felt like coming home or stepping back into a nightmare. I took a deep breath and swallowed. There was only one way to find out.

ith only a day to go before filming, the tent was buzzing with activity. A cleaning crew, cameramen, and what looked to be a new sound guy were going about their duties with a quiet intensity. I optimistically scanned the tent for Elspeth or Gina, but no such luck. Worse luck, in fact, as I spied Gerry in the corner hovering over the ovens and admonishing Aaron Keel, the electrician, who was checking the wiring. For a scary second, I thought Aaron might have heard Gerry because he straightened and looked suspiciously around. But it must have been instinct, not ability, that he sensed someone flapping around in his face.

Waving to a couple of the cameramen, I gestured to my bag of goodies and went to my workstation. Its white surface was sparkling. I carefully put the gooseberries and eggs into the fridge and the honey in my allocated cupboard, closing the door gently. My mind began to whir with ideas on how to make my gooseberry upside-down cake sing tomorrow.

When I came out of the tent, I saw Peter Puddifoot walking down the path from the manor house. He did not look like he was in a good mood. When he looked up and saw me staring, he glared until I hastily averted my gaze. He didn't know I'd overheard his argument with Arnold Bentley or that I knew he believed he should have had Broomewode Farm. I wondered if he'd been up at the big house complaining about the current farm tenants. If he had, he didn't look like his visit had been a success.

He made his way toward a riding lawnmower, climbed aboard and started it up with a roar. I watched him attacking the lawn as though each blade of grass was his enemy and he was leaving no prisoners. The sound was deafening.

I made a wide berth, not wishing to be mistaken for lawn.

Suddenly, he stopped, got down, and walked around the front of his lawnmower with a frown on his face. He bent and picked something up, turning it in his hands. I moved closer. It was Sly's orange ball. As if on cue, the collie came bounding across the freshly mowed grass, kicking up green as he went. But as he got closer, I saw Peter's face turn redder and redder. He was furious. The collie bounded up to his ball and tried to jump up to Peter to say hello—but to my absolute horror, Peter's foot shot out. I watched it happen in slow motion. The boot. The happy dog's face. And then the impact. Sly yelped and fell back.

I was horrified and cried out, running forward.

Once more the gardener glared at me. "Keep this bloody dog off my lawn," he shouted. He must know perfectly well it wasn't my dog. He threw the ball on the ground in disgust and stomped back to his mower.

Sly picked up his ball, and I grabbed his collar and walked awkwardly away, bent over, my arm like a human leash.

When we were well out of lawnmower range, I stopped and crouched in front of the dog. "Poor thing," I murmured, stroking his head, while his big brown eyes stared at me adoringly. "You didn't do anything wrong." That hateful Peter. Did he kick the dog as a way of getting back at its owner? What kind of a monster would do something like that?

I wanted to stand up for this loyal dog who'd saved my life, but I didn't know what to do. Go and tell Lord Frome what his gardener was up to? Give the grumpy gardener a piece of my mind? I felt a chill down the back of my neck and turned to see Gerry behind my shoulder. "Did you see that? He kicked poor Sly." I was furious but still kept my head enough to make sure I kept looking at the collie. Let anyone watching think I was talking to the dog.

"I did," he said. "Peter Puddifoot is a right rotter. You do not want to rub that geezer up the wrong way."

A cameraman was coming toward us, and I couldn't be seen talking to nothing, so I told Sly to go back home (to my surprise, he licked my hand, took his ball and then dashed off) and then started to walk down a quieter path.

"Hey! *Ruuuude.* Where do you think you're going?" Gerry whined.

I made a small follow-me motion with my hand and kept walking.

"Ah, I get it. You don't wanna look like you've lost the plot talking to thin air." He sighed and put a hand through his belly. "Can't believe this bad boy isn't solid. All those hours in the gym. And now no one can see my perfect abs."

We were far away enough now that I could reply. "Gerry, you were more sweet doughnut than rock candy and you know it."

He laughed good-naturedly. "No point going to the gym now. What you see is what you get."

I turned onto the gravel path back to the inn. I checked that no one was around and then said, "So tell me, what on earth is Peter's problem?"

"Well, one benefit to being a ghost is I get to overhear private conversations. And what a corker I witnessed earlier this week. Puddifoot and a chap named Arnold had a huge fight and—"

"Wait, did you say Arnold?"

He nodded.

"Arnold Bentley?"

"No idea of his surname. Old geezer, long face and looked like he was headed to his gentlemen's club fifty years too late."

I smiled, but the description was perfect. "I met him today."

"Those two had a massive argument over the grounds of Broomewode Hall a couple of days back. Turns out that Lord Frome had promised Arnold that his team of gardeners would also look after part of the Bentley's farmland. But Peter and his team had been slacking off, deciding that it wasn't part of their job to please their boss's mates. But when Arnold came to the inn to ask Peter about it this week, Peter just exploded about 'not bending to the will of privileged tossers.'"

"So that's two massive arguments the two have had." I filled Gerry in on the fight I'd overheard.

He whistled softly. "No wonder he's got such a bug up his arse. He thought the farm was going to be his. Now, not only does he lose the farm but also his pet bees."

I turned to him, astonished. "Pet bees? Who kicks a beautiful dog and fights for stinging insects?"

"Tells you everything you need to know about Peter Puddifoot."

I thought of that beautiful, golden honey and felt horrible. "Bees are wonderful insects. They pollinate flowers and make honey and wax. I don't mean to be unkind."

He looked at me oddly. "Poppy, I don't think they can hear you." He leaned closer and in a stage whisper said, "You didn't hurt the bees' feelings."

I laughed. "I do think Peter Puddifoot's feelings, if he has any, have been hurt, though. He really has it in for Arnold Bentley. Which I don't really care about, but he was unkind to the best dog in the world."

I TOLD him about my visit to Broomewode Farm and once more recounted the tale of the falling tower stone.

"Blimey," Gerry said when I'd finished. "Not that I don't want the company, Pops, but you should be more careful."

"I never thought of picking fruit as a dangerous activity before today."

Before Gerry could answer, the sound of muttering reached us. It was a man's voice, but I couldn't work out what he was saying.

"Better dash," Gerry said. "Don't want you getting caught talking to yourself."

I raised my eyebrows, surprised at Gerry's thoughtfulness. He grinned and drifted back toward the tent. "Think I'll go haunt that useless electrician again."

I continued along the gravel path back toward the inn. The beds of white and blue hyacinths on either side of me emitted their scent, and I breathed deeply. I had to calm down, forget falling stones and dog-kicking gardeners. Think about gooseberry cakes instead.

The muttering was getting louder, but I still couldn't work out where it was coming from. I turned off the path in the direction of the rose garden, and that's when I realized the voice was familiar. Very familiar.

"The perfect fruit cake is tricky because the fruit will make the batter heavy if the baker's overloading it. You must adjust the amounts of flour and liquid depending on the juiciness of the fruit."

Was that Jonathon, reciting lines? I paused to listen further and accidentally kicked a bit of gravel.

"Hello?" he called. "Someone there?"

I emerged from behind a rose bush and there was Jonathon, sitting on a bench. In his lap was an open book, and he slammed it shut the second he saw me. The cover was as familiar to me as my own face. Jonathon was reciting from his own recipe book.

"Hi," I said. "Sorry to interrupt you."

Jonathon looked sheepish. "Busted, huh. I know I might appear as if I was born to be on screen, but I get nervous under pressure, too, just like you bakers. So I thought I'd memorize some of my own descriptions so I sound more...relaxed."

Ha, born to be on screen? *Vain much, Jonathon?*

I laughed. "Your little secret is safe with me. I won't tell anyone you need to memorize your own recipes even though you wrote them in the first place."

I expected Jonathon to laugh, but he didn't react at all. His usually lively blue eyes were flat and hard to read. I stepped back nervously. I hadn't really spoken with Jonathon since Elspeth had told me that he was a witch, too. I wasn't sure if he knew that I was a witch or whether *he* knew that *I* knew he was one. What were the rules here? I had no idea. So I decided to follow my mom and dad's favorite mantra, which was, when in doubt, do nothing.

"I'll leave you to it, then, shall I?" He still looked stern, so I went with flattery. He was one of the judges, after all. "I almost have some of your recipes memorized too. The salted caramel bread and butter pudding is my favorite."

He smiled at last. "Oh yeah, that one is delicious for sure."

Phew. Good recovery. The last thing I needed was a black mark against my name with one of the judges of the show. I told him that I was heading back to the inn to get some lunch, as though I somehow needed his permission.

When I rounded a bend in the path, I heard him say, "The finest ingredients will make for superior taste."

Having nearly died in pursuit of the finest local ingredients, I hoped he remembered those words tomorrow.

BACK AT THE PUB, there were only a few people sitting at tables, and I suspected they were with the production. The lone man from earlier was tucking into a sandwich. Next to his plate, steam was rising from a cup of coffee. He and Eve were chatting away. Which was annoying, as I wanted to chat with Eve.

I pulled out a barstool and took a seat right at the bar. Eve must have taken the hint, for she soon came over. She took one look at me and handed me a menu before she even said hello. I thanked her and scanned the options before settling on a cheese baguette with a side of triple-cooked fries.

"You all right, Poppy? You look a little pale."

I opened my mouth, about to tell Eve all about my second close call with the grim reaper that week, but then decided against it. I wasn't entirely sure why. Maybe I didn't want to become someone who other people thought attracted danger. "Yes. Just hungry." I shifted the conversation to the pub. "Tell me about Peter Puddifoot."

She paused, suddenly going still. "The gardener?"

No. The earl. "Yes, the gardener."

She picked up a cloth and began to polish the bar top as though the health inspector was on their way. "He's a local lad. Grew up here."

That was it? For a woman who liked to talk as much as Eve did, that wasn't very much information. I decided to tell her about the fight I'd overheard. She didn't look very surprised. "And then he kicked Arnold Bentley's dog. What kind of a person kicks a dog?"

She heaved a sigh. "A very angry person." She'd stopped scrubbing the bar's surface and was only wiping absentmindedly. "That argument you overheard? He's not lying. The Puddifoot family has farmed Broomewode Farm for generations. Peter fully expected to take over when his father died. He was the one who started keeping bees. He was much happier in those days. When his father died, it shocked everyone that the new earl rented the farm to the Bentleys."

I was a little sympathetic that he'd had his home pulled out from under him, but I didn't think it gave him an excuse to kick dogs and glare at innocent bakers. I could see that she wanted to say more but was no doubt sensitive to the fact that Broomewode Hall and the Champneys paid her wages. "Well, there was no excuse to kick at a dog."

"Absolutely right. None at all."

We were agreed on that, then. My sandwich arrived and I tucked into it. The fries were crisp and crunchy, exactly the way I liked them.

"How's business? Is everyone in this pub with the TV production?"

SHE GLANCED AROUND. "Mostly. Not the one sitting by the fireplace, though." She gestured to the man she'd been chatting to. "Bob Fielding is a car tire salesman. Special tires for four by fours. Very la-di-da. He's got it into his head that the country folk round here, the Champneys in particular, are the perfect market for his wares."

I had never heard the words tires and la-di-da used in the same sentence before. "There are tires expensive enough to support a traveling salesman?"

"Oh, yes." Eve's eyes darted around the room, and then she leaned across the bar conspiratorially, dropping her voice to a whisper. "But he's wasting his time. The Champneys haven't got money for fancy-pants car tires. Or anything else, for that matter."

"What do you mean?" I whispered back, incredulous. "The TV production must bring in a fortune?"

Eve solemnly shook her head. "Lord and Lady Frome spend it faster than they can make it. Besides, I heard a rumor that they made some very bad investments." She looked around the room again. "They don't come from money, you see."

I didn't understand. The Champneys were titled people, esteemed members of the aristocracy. I didn't have a lot of money myself, so it wasn't like I was an expert on the subject, but I did know that cash stuck to those who already had it. And how could you have a title without a little dough to your name?

Eve poured herself a soda water and squeezed a wedge of lime into the glass. "Seeing as it's not busy, let me tell you a little story," she said. And what came next shocked me almost as much as learning that Jonathon had to memorize his own recipes.

"Lord Frome wasn't the next in line when it came to inheriting his title. He was the cousin of the man who should have inherited. The original heir was a healthy and strong chap in his twenties, known for his prowess as an amateur boxer, as much as his aristocratic family. It was before my time, but he was well liked, well connected, well educated. I heard that he was very good-looking and everyone was waiting for him to marry some debutante and start his own family. He had some lovely girlfriends. They used to have their photos in *The Tattler*. But sadly, it wasn't meant to be."

Here she paused to take a drink, and I held my breath. Ooh, she really was a good storyteller.

"He was riding around the property as he'd done a thousand times. But he was thrown off his horse at the worst possible spot, thrown right over the side of a cliff. Killed instantly. Sadly, he was the only child and the one who was born and bred to be the earl. Everyone round here says that he'd have made a better job of it than these two if he'd been given half the chance. The current earl wasn't bred to it, you see. He makes mistakes."

"Whoa," I said. "That's terrible. Poor guy. What a way to go—and so young, too." I started to feel that rather than being a good energy vortex, Broomewode might be more of tragedy vortex.

"Their son, Ben, seems to have a better sense of the land, but then he's spent most of his life here. We have high hopes for him."

Well, Ben hadn't been romancing debutantes today. He'd been mending fences. I only hoped he'd remembered to put the warning signs up and roped off the dangerous area around the ruined chapel.

"Poppy? There you are."

I turned on my barstool. Elspeth! She looked as wonderful as ever in a pair of soft black slacks and elegant white shirt, a single string of pearls at her neck.

She greeted me with two swift kisses to my cheeks before pulling away with a worried expression on her face. "I was wondering if I could have a quick word."

No, *Lovely to see you* or a simple *How you doing, Poppy?* Was everything always going to be urgent and worrying now that I was a witch?

Eve raised a quizzical eyebrow, and I excused myself. Elspeth led us to a table in the corner.

"You're kind of scaring me, Elspeth," I said as we sat down.

"Oh dear, Poppy, sorry, that's the last thing I want. Did something happen? It's just that I felt you were in great danger. And I'm so pleased to see you safe."

She put her hand over mine, and a sense of calm settled over my jangled senses, like when you rub a cool healing gel on a burn.

I told her about what had happened at the tower earlier, and her kind gray eyes grew wide with alarm. "My goodness. You have to be so careful, Poppy," she chided.

"Why? Why do you always say that to me? How dangerous is it to go picking fruit?"

"And yet you nearly died," she said softly.

"But it was an accident. That ancient tower looks like it's been crumbling for years. Centuries probably."

"I'm going to give you a protection spell. You must recite it every night when you go to bed and every morning when you wake up. It will help protect against all harm. Accidental and otherwise."

A spell? I already had a cat, a dog, a ghost, and a special amethyst necklace looking out for me. Team Poppy was getting crowded.

"I'll bring it to your room a bit later."

I didn't want to hurt her feelings, but I hoped her protection spell was stronger than the amethyst necklace.

Loud laughter and greetings of *Hello, hello* and *How are you* floated from the inn's hallway into the pub. Elspeth rose and told me she'd have to leave before the other contestants spotted us together. She didn't want them thinking she had favorites.

"What time tonight? Do I need to prepare?"

At that, Elspeth just smiled a small smile and smoothed down her slacks. "Have a bath, relax and try to clear your mind. We'll talk later, my dear."

Clear my mind? Easy for her to say. I wished it was that easy to forget the horror of the morning.

A moment or two after Elspeth left, Gaurav and Priscilla arrived. I tried to mimic a woman who had nothing more serious on her mind than competitive baking, stood and walked to where my fellow contestants were greeting Eve.

"Poppy," Priscilla said, giving me a hug. "How funny. Gaurav and I were just saying how we didn't expect to see anyone else here this early. But now there are three of us. I guess we all had the same idea about getting settled ahead of schedule."

I smiled at Priscilla, surprised at the hug. We hadn't gotten the chance to speak much last week, but she seemed as pleased to see me as if we'd been best friends. I guess everything that had happened had made the group bond faster. Gaurav said he'd taken a holiday day. He was a research scientist from Birmingham, and Priscilla was a hairdresser from Leeds. They'd both brought special produce to make their cakes and, like me, had wanted time to prepare themselves mentally as well as physically for the weekend.

For now, I wanted to excuse myself and have some alone time. I'd only been back half a day, and so much had happened already.

However, before I got to the bottom of the stairs, Florence arrived, looking as glamorous as though she were a movie star turning up to an awards show. And one day, I suspected she would be exactly that. She created a sort of buzz when she arrived. Not only was she beautiful, but she had a way of drawing attention.

She'd also decided we would be friends, and before I

could slip away to my room, there was a giant squeal. "Poppy!"

Florence rushed toward me, her long, auburn curls bouncing and her white teeth on full display, and flung herself into my arms. I would have burst out laughing at the over-the-top *Romeo and Juliet*-style dramatics of it all, but I was too crushed to even breathe. Finally, she pulled away and looked at me. "What a pretty color that gloss is on you," she said, smiling.

Maggie, the grandmother who was one of the strongest bakers on the show, arrived at the same time. She came over and gave me a more reserved version of Florence's hug. It was so good to see them both. The three of us walked into the pub all talking at once. Gaurav and Priscilla raised their hands in hello.

Florence, without even asking, somehow had Gaurav carry her very heavy cases up to her room. She'd packed even more than I had for a weekend. "Now don't go anywhere, Poppy," she ordered. "I'm just going to change my shoes, and then we must walk into town. The little delicatessen here ordered in the special flour I like from Milano. I must pick it up for tomorrow."

"But we're supposed to highlight local produce," I reminded her.

She waved an airy hand. "Yes, yes. I have lovely little British strawberries, but for the cake, I must have the Italian flour. Your British flour is too cakey."

I had no idea why that was a bad thing when one was baking a cake, but we all had our quirks. If Florence believed Italian flour would give her a slight edge in the competition, I completely understood why she'd order it in specially.

So, in a very few minutes, she came back down the stairs. As well as changing her shoes, she'd also managed to freshen her makeup and brush her hair. She looked stunning.

Florence and I walked into the small town of Broomewode. It was one of those tiny, charming villages that are almost too pretty to be real. Many of the houses had stood there for hundreds of years, and even the newer builds were made of the same local stone so there was a unified feel to the whole. The shopping area of the high street looked like a postcard. No traffic was allowed on the cobbled street.

Down the median were flower displays that also acted as bollards, no doubt to prevent misguided motorists or skateboarders from heading down the middle of the road. On either side were little shops with flats above. There was a bookshop, a baker, a butcher, a delicatessen, a real estate agent, a charity shop and several cafes.

Florence was easy company. She loved to talk and always had stories about auditions she'd been to, parties she'd attended, the new play she'd seen in the West End. She was content to talk, needing very little encouragement from me, which allowed me to listen with half my concentration while mulling things with the other half. She added so much drama to her recital that even a boring dinner sounded like a Shakespeare tragedy. She had me laughing about how she had been forced to eat a badly cooked dessert. "No, really, Poppy. Don't laugh. I am Italian and a contestant on the baking show, and they made me tiramisu. First, no British person should be allowed to make tiramisu, and second, they shouldn't be allowed to feed it to an Italian like myself with a sensitive palate."

We entered the delicatessen, and within seconds she and

the owner were happily conversing in Italian. I poked around, enjoying browsing everything from Genoa salami to Gorgonzola cheese, to packaged pasta and about thirty varieties of olive oil. Just breathing in made me hungry, and I was delighted when the owner offered us both a tiny almond cake.

He presented Florence with her flour, and we both bought some dried fruit and nuts. If I didn't use it in my baking, I could always snack on the fruits and nuts.

With lots of cheek-kissing and *ciao-ciaos,* we walked out again onto the pretty street. "Shall we walk back another way?" she suggested. She pointed down another road. "I think that will take us back to the pub a longer way, and it's such a nice afternoon, we might as well enjoy it."

I was happy to explore, so we headed to the village green, where a pair of spaniels played while their owners chatted, and through it to a street of houses. We passed a charity shop that I'd have to come back and check out when I had more time. There were some very old pieces of china and crockery that I thought would look good in my kitchen at home.

We were still in the old town, and many of the stone cottages already sported hanging baskets, while their front gardens were bright and fragrant with spring blooms. After the charity shop and a small corner store, we entered a more residential area.

Florence continued talking as we walked along the quiet village street.

I noticed a sign for Broomewode Smithy. This must be where the fireplace tools and other ironwork were made that were featured in the gift shop. From the age of the stone house, it had stood there for centuries. I wondered if the artisan blacksmith still used the old forge. While I admired the wonderful old building, a woman and a man came out of the front door and onto the front porch. They stood quite close to each other, talking intensely. I stopped dead and couldn't seem to look away. Florence got two steps ahead of me before she realized I wasn't with her and returned to my side. She followed my gaze. "What is it? It's just a husband saying goodbye to his wife."

But it wasn't. The woman standing so close to the man was Susan Bentley. The man was a stranger to me. He was quite the silver fox. Tall, with a full head of silver-gray hair and a nice profile. He had the kind of build that suggested he worked out or had been an athlete.

I took Florence's arm, and we walked on a few steps while I considered what she'd said. "What made you think they were husband and wife?"

I suspected her thoughts had already moved on because she looked puzzled for a second before realizing what I was talking about. "You mean those two back there?" She stopped to think. "The way they stood so close to each other, I suppose. There was real affection there. I think if we'd stayed staring, we'd have seen him kiss her goodbye. Why do you ask?"

I didn't want to tell the truth, that that woman was married to another man, so I merely said, "It's interesting the way you read people so well. I imagine it's because you're an actress."

It was the perfect thing to say, for Florence was quite willing to expand in great detail on how she studied people in order to become a better actress. By the time she'd moved on to how she used the Alexander breathing technique, I was wondering if she could be right about the couple. They weren't married, but they could be lovers.

I had liked Susan Bentley very much, more than I'd enjoyed meeting her husband. I had no idea what was going on in the Bentley marriage, but I thought it was a bit shameless of Susan Bentley to be seen coming out of another man's house in the middle of the afternoon in such a small village. I wondered who the man was and if their affair was the talk of the town.

By the time we got back, nearly everyone had arrived. I spotted Daniel, the dentist; Amara, the doctor; and Evie, the NHS administrator, talking together in the corner.

There was no sign of Euan or Hamish yet, but I was sure they'd be there soon.

Then there was a giant sneeze, and Hamish entered the room. "Oh lordy," he said in his Scottish accent. "I've caught a terrible chill. Can't seem to shake this blasted cold. Been in bed all week."

The entire room jumped back. No one wanted to be ill at such a crucial time.

"All right, all right," Hamish muttered, raising his hands in mock surrender. "No need for that. I'm over the worst of it, and I've got a big bottle of antibacterial gel practically glued to my side if anyone's worried."

Florence shot me a look and whispered devilishly, "I hope it's man flu. Nothing worse."

Everyone ordered drinks from Eve, and the group clinked glasses, happy to be back and hopeful for a normal weekend of baking antics. Euan finally arrived after getting a flat tire, and we all sat down to eat. The Friday night special was roast lemon chicken, roast potatoes, and buttery spring greens. As I tucked into my piled-high plate, I took a moment to be thankful, truly thankful to be alive, and back at Broomewode—the place I knew was going to connect me with my birth family.

WE ALL DECIDED on an early night, knowing tomorrow would be full on. As instructed by Elspeth, I poured myself a bath and had a good, long soak. After my bath, I wanted to get into my pajamas and slip into bed with a cookbook, but Elspeth had said she'd be by to do a protection spell, so I dressed instead in gray sweats. I brushed out my long, brown hair and tied it in a ponytail to keep it out of the way.

I felt a bit nervous. I wasn't sure about having a witch put a spell on me, even if that witch was the great Elspeth Peach. I decided to settle on my bed with my cookbook and try to relax.

When I heard scratching at my window, I sat bold upright in bed, startled. It took a moment before I remembered that I was back at the inn, not in my cottage, and that I must have fallen asleep. I'd been dreaming about burning a salted caramel sauce. Not even my dreams were safe from cake-related disasters.

"Gateau, there you are," I cooed, lifting the sash window to let her in. She squeezed through the gap and leapt onto my bed. Outside, the moon was almost full. I could just see the outline of the tower in the distance. I put a hand to my necklace and said a thank-you to Sly for protecting me and decided that I'd see if Eve would have a word with the pub cook and save a really juicy bone for Sly.

Heavy boots clomped along the hallway outside, followed

by the whir of suitcases being wheeled. Someone else was arriving. Or leaving.

Gateau, who needed no encouragement, was already asleep, nestled into my bed cover.

There was a soft knock on my door, and there was Elspeth. She came in, looked pleased to see Gateau and shut the door behind her. She looked her impeccable self. No one would ever guess that this well-dressed celebrity was a witch. But, as she unpacked the tote bag she'd brought with her, she became more witchlike. She had candles, a vial of tiny crystals, and a pretty bottle that should have held perfume but I was guessing didn't.

"Right," she said, rubbing her hands together. "All the ingredients are assembled. Now, come and stand here." She chose a spot in the room where the moonlight streamed in. "Good. A nice clear night." She pushed an armchair out of the way, and I stood where I was told.

She set out candles in a circle around me, then sprinkled the crystals. "It's only salt, dear. A special kind." She stepped closer, holding the perfume bottle. "And now we cast our circle." She spoke as though she were explaining how to make the perfect muffin.

Gateau had been watching from half-slit eyes. Now she hopped off the bed and came to join us in the circle. Elspeth pointed at the first candle and muttered something. It jumped to life. Honestly, I wasn't even shocked. She proceeded to light the rest of the candles with no need of matches or lighter. Then she turned to me. She uncorked the bottle, and I could smell something spicy but pleasant. She tipped a little on her finger, and I saw it was some kind of oil. First she dabbed a bit on the amethyst. Was it like a battery that had lost its charge and needed a reboot? Then, she dabbed oil on my forehead and the dip of my collarbone while saying the following:

Earth, Fire, Water, all three,
Elements of Astral, I summon thee,
By the moon's light
On this special night
I call to thee to give us your might
By the power of three
I conjure thee
To protect our sweet Poppy
And all that surrounds she
So I will, so mote it be
So I will, so mote it be.

I felt a shiver run down my back, but that could simply have been nerves. Gateau rubbed up against my legs as though telling me everything would be fine.

Elspeth said, "And now our circle's done," and the candles went out as easily as they'd lighted themselves.

"How do you feel?" she asked me.

"No different."

"You must still be vigilant, my dear, but this spell should help ward off evil."

Well, that was good. Attracting evil wasn't really part of my life plan.

CHAPTER 6

The tent glowed white with studio lights, illuminating the setting for *The Great British Baking Contest,* just as I'd remembered it. The six cameras were positioned for action, crew poised. Rows of pristine workstations were set at intervals from each other, ready and waiting to receive spilled flour and egg across their shiny surfaces. And then I realized there *was* something different about the tent: there were only ten workstations, two fewer than last week, two less contestants.

I'd all but forgotten about Marcus pulling out of the show last minute. And no one had even brought him up at dinner last night. Turns out that behaving like a spoiled baby really did make you forgettable. But not even the memory of that sourpuss could spoil the excitement that was gurgling away in my belly. I was nervous (of course) but also eager to get going and use the amazing ingredients that Susan gifted me yesterday. Without even cracking a happy egg, I knew that their yolks would be gloriously orange, rich and delicious. Fresh farm eggs like those were like gold dust for a cake, and I couldn't wait to show off my gooseberry knowledge to the camera—that is, if I managed to somehow keep my cool and not stumble over my words, or be a klutz and knock a bowl of flour over Jilly or Arty. Ooh, and now I remembered the sweet (or not so sweet) embrace I saw the night of Gerry's murder. I wondered if those two would officially announce they were a couple or if it'd been a reaction to the drama of the day. But before I pondered the romantic decisions of two comedians, Donald Friesen, the series producer, walked on to the set, and the buzzing and muttering of crew and cast fell silent. If I didn't know better, I'd have thought it was Donald, not Jonathon, who was the real witch, getting a room to hush like that.

Ever the showman, Donald welcomed us back and said we had great team spirit. Gerry suddenly appeared at my side. "Ha. He should try being a real spirit."

"Now. Just a reminder that the cameras will move around and you should pretend they're not even there, except when you put anything into your oven or take it out. We always want to film those wonderful moments." He cleared his throat and motioned a young guy with a beard and glasses forward. "Everyone, I want you to meet Robbie Denton. He'll be your soundman. Do make him welcome."

As an awkward silence descended, Priscilla waved. "Hiya."

"That's it?" Gerry said, sounding put out. "That's all Donald has to say? What about, 'This one's not a murdering nutter. We hope. Or, hard luck, Gerry.' In fact, would a minute of silence have been too much to ask in memory of my unfortunate demise? Where's the respect?"

I felt for him, I really did, but I couldn't talk to thin air.

Luckily, Robbie, the new sound guy, was approaching, so I gave Gerry a sympathetic glance and kept my mouth shut.

Robbie Denton seemed like a nice enough guy in his mid-twenties. I suspected he wore the full beard to try and appear older. "Hello," he said as he approached. "You're Poppy."

I smiled at him, feeling how nervous he was. "That's right."

"I tried to memorize everyone's name. It's always a bit difficult on the first day."

"You'll do fine." Being an improvement over Gordon wasn't much of a stretch. All he had to do was not kill anyone.

He went around getting each of us mic'd up while the cameras got into position and everything was checked. A few nervous coughs interrupted the quiet. Then Fiona, the director, stepped up and it was lights, camera, action.

Jonathon and Elspeth walked into the tent, gliding together with steps in perfect sync. As ever, I was wowed by Elspeth's glamour, which worked well against Jonathon's tough exterior. I smoothed down my apron and rearranged the line of my shirt. I'd chosen my outfit with Gina earlier. She'd snuck into my room this morning after breakfast, on a quick break from setting up her hair and make-up station and rifled through my selection of blouses and tops. Eventually, after she'd dismissed several options, Gina settled on a warm orange silk shirt, saying that it brought out the chestnut tones in my hair. I didn't care if that was true or not. I was going to believe it. She'd done my makeup to match, coral eye shadow and a nude lipstick, and the denim skirt she paired it all with was comfortable yet stylish. To finish it all off, she lent me a pair of her oversize gold earrings. I didn't usually wear much jewelry, but these gorgeous hoops really made the outfit. I knew I could count on Gina.

Elspeth caught my eye and sent a discreet smile my way. I touched the amethyst necklace and hoped that as well as protecting me, it could protect my cake from burning.

Florence waved at me. She looked every part the Hollywood bombshell in a ruffled black cotton dress. Her red hair was perfectly curled and swept away from her face with the help of a few deft bobby pins. Already, we were each developing a signature style. She was the gorgeous starlet, I was the girl next door, Maggie was the kind grandmother, Hamish the solid Scottish policeman, Euan the gentle Welsh beekeeper, Amara the refined doctor, Priscilla was slightly goofy, and Gaurav serious, and somewhat shy while Evie was outgoing and emotional. Daniel. How to describe Daniel? The family guy.

The cameras trained on Jonathon's face, and his usual serious expression bloomed into a warm smile. He cleared his throat and introduced the first challenge.

"Bakers, how lovely it is to see you all back here this week. And still smiling."

There was a ripple of laughter that Donald encouraged from the sidelines.

"This week is one of my personal favorites: cake week. And your first challenge is to bake a fruit cake using seasonal British fruits. Now, you should all know that the perfect fruit cake is tricky because the fruit will make the batter heavy if the baker's overloading it. You must adjust the amounts of flour and liquid depending on the juiciness of the fruit."

Wowzers. Jonathon really did learn his lines thoroughly. That was word for word what I'd overheard in the rose garden. I tuned out of what Jonathon said next and instead stole a look around the room. Did everyone else feel the same mix of excitement and fear? Amara looked stern and focused; Hamish was sneezing into a white handkerchief, poor guy. Maggie had an angelic smile on her kind face; Daniel was totally beaming, bursting to go. Our expressions told the story of our hopes and fears. I swallowed hard and hoped that I could keep it together and bake my little butt off.

Before I knew it, Jonathon was announcing that the first challenge was about to start, and the timers were set.

The comedians came forward, made some joke about fruit cake, but I felt so nervous, the words sailed past until I heard Jilly say, "On your marks, get set, bake!"

I did the exact thing we were told not to do and stared right at the camera that was pointing at me like a nosy neighbor. I was immediately flustered and tried to act competent. What was I supposed to be doing? The ingredients, the method—everything flew completely out of my head. Bye. Bye. Recipe. But then I saw a friendly face urging me on by flapping his hands about manically. Gerry. Ah, my ghostly cheerleader, doing a dance at the entrance of the tent. He zoomed up to me. "Come on, Pops, pull it together."

"Can't think what to do first," I muttered. If cameras were on me it would look like I was talking to myself. Or praying.

Gerry bent bonelessly over, stretching his body ludicrously so he could see my recipe. "First up, cream the butter and sugar. You could do this in your sleep. You've got to get your focus back, girl."

I thought he was being so nice until he continued, "You're the only one who can see me. If you get sent home, I'll be bored stupid. Now focus."

Maybe he was only thinking of his ghostly self, but his pep talk helped. He was right. I knew this recipe. Plus, since I'd nearly died collecting the gooseberries, I was determined to get a good cake out of them.

I tipped the two ingredients into a glass bowl and got to work. When the mix became fluffy and light, I began to add the eggs and part of the flour. This was more like it. I was in the zone. "Atta girl," a voice said. I turned, and Gerry was floating behind me. I had to swallow hard to avoid batting him away. He knew I couldn't react to anything he said or did without looking like the pressure had made me crack. Why couldn't he stick to cheering me on from a distance? Luckily, Arty chose that moment to get chatting, and Gerry took the hint and drifted away.

"Hello, Poppy," he said. "A little birdy told me that you're making a gooseberry cake. What made you go with such a *tart* fruit? Are you trying to tell us something?"

I blushed. Jilly saved me from replying. "Who are you calling a tart?" She took over. "It's very early for gooseberries, isn't it?"

I shuddered, once more thinking I'd nearly died trying to pick the freakishly early fruit.

"It is early, but I stumbled on a patch that were sunning themselves in a nice, secluded spot. I love gooseberries. Get the balance right when cooking, and they'll have that wonderful sweet and sour taste. Here, I'm making an upside-down cake, and I'll be adding some raspberry meringue kisses, too. Pairing tart gooseberries with raspberries means that the sponge will have sweetness, sourness and texture, with pockets of moist fruit in every mouthful," I said. Whoa. Did I sound professional or what? I'd borrowed Jonathon's trick and had written down and memorized a few key phrases. It worked.

"Raspberry kisses, eh? Someone really is feeling fruity. I think these gooseberries come from somewhere *very* close to home?"

I was so glad I'd told everyone that the gooseberries were from Broomewode Farm. Now, I didn't even have to clumsily introduce that fact myself. I carried on beating my mix and replied, "That's right. They're from Broomewode Farm, which is just the other side of the manor house. The Bentleys, who run the farm, also provided the free-range eggs and a pot of their golden honey. I picked the gooseberries myself." I hoped my shudder wouldn't show on camera when I recalled how close I'd come to being gooseberry jam myself.

"When they said local produce, you really stuck to the brief." The jar of honey was still on my workstation, and I was pleased that the camera came in for a close-up. Maybe the footage would be cut, but at least I'd tried to give Susan Bentley a bit of free advertising.

Jilly picked up a few of the berries and studied them. "They aren't very pretty, though, are they? And 'playing gooseberry' is considered an insult."

"Gooseberries are underrated. They have many healing properties. They're high in fiber, rich in antioxidants such as phytonutrients and vitamins E and C, which may help protect your brain and fight aging and many types of diseases." I went on to explain the history Susan had told me about their origins from India and medicinal properties. Once more, I was repeating what I'd memorized, and thank you, Jonathon, for the idea.

"Blimey," Arty exclaimed. "I had no idea those tiny green guys could do so much."

I laughed, and Arty thanked me and went to speak to Florence.

Florence had ditched the strawberries and was making a rhubarb cake. Like the gooseberries, it had grown early this year and her new Italian friend from the deli had brought some over first thing this morning, picked fresh. She'd sweetened the fruit with a sticky elderflower cordial, and the delicious smell was traveling my way. At least I'd remembered to eat a big breakfast this morning. There was no chance of me becoming distracted by getting peckish.

I stopped beating for a moment and watched how natural Florence was in front of the camera. She was so warm and confident. A born cookery show host. Her nails this week were an eggplant-black, and they caught the light as she furiously hand-whisked her mix. Even as she raved about the local rhubarb, she managed to slip in that her flour was specially imported from Italy. I could relax now that I'd said my piece and remembered everything I'd so carefully planned.

I got back to my batter. Next I had to place the gooseberries in their honey syrup in the pre-lined tin before covering it with the sponge mix. Then, camera trained on me, I slid the tin into the oven. Phew. I took a moment to wish my baking well, just like always.

I cleaned up my messy workstation and surveyed what everyone else was up to. Using seasonal ingredients was one of my favorite things to do in baking, but Britain didn't have the best selection at this time of year. It was a tougher challenge than it seemed. I saw that Amara and Euan had played it safe and were using strawberries, but Amara really stood out with her inventive twist of flavoring the berries with pink peppercorns. It was such a cool combination. I wanted to try a mouthful myself.

I wasn't the only one using honey. Hamish was doing something super clever by incorporating parsnips into his cake, sweetened with honey, and topping it off with an elder-flower cream-cheese frosting. I was intrigued, but it sounded like there might be too much going on there, flavor-wise. It was a bold move. I guess he'd gained a bit of confidence. Now that we were in our second week, people were getting into their stride. Personally, now that I'd accepted that I was *actually* part of a TV show that *actual* people were going to watch, I now couldn't help but imagine what the voiceover might be saying as they edited our cooking segments. Was the voice explaining what makes a good sponge? Where we all might be going wrong but didn't know it yet? It was difficult to gauge what the scene looked like when you were baking your heart out.

I prepared to make some raspberry meringues, or "kisses," as I was calling them, to decorate the outside of my cake. I separated the yolks and whites from six more of my happy eggs and put the whites, along with sugar, into the mixer. I set it to low and watched the mix like a hawk, waiting for stiff peaks to form that would still have a little bit of movement. When the whip was right, I crushed some freeze-dried raspberries, put the mix through a sieve, and then stirred the sweet fruity powder into the meringue. With the help of a pipe, I styled the meringue mix into little 'kisses' on a tray and then put the lot into the oven for thirty-five minutes.

I checked on the sponge. It still had a bit of a shake in the middle, and I was scared if I took it out now, then the sponge would collapse when I flipped it. I'd know when it was ready when it didn't shake. But even just a minute over that moment, and the sponge would start to dry out. Oven timing was critical. I had to get it absolutely spot on, otherwise my sponge would be liquid or the fruit would be overdone.

"Oh no!" a voice cried out. When I turned, I saw Priscilla shaking her head at the oven. "It's bubbling in there. Bubbling like a *volcano*. It shouldn't be doing that. I don't know what to do?"

She looked ready to grab her tin out of the oven. Hamish stopped what he was doing and went over to help, peering through the glass door into her oven. "You're fine. You're fine. That's the syrup inside getting hot. Don't worry, my darlin', it's going to be okay."

"Ooh, I hope so, lovey," she said, sticking her hands out in front of her. "Look at me. I'm shaking." Naturally, a camera was trained on them. Those were the moments everyone loved. It was always my favorite part when I used to watch the baking contest. Back when I could be an armchair baker and judge. Oh, those were the days.

Hamish put a friendly arm around her shoulders and walked her back to her workstation top. "You just concentrate on your topping now. Stay focused. You've got this."

I smiled. It was so nice when we helped each other. Unlike last week, with Marcus and Gerry's macho standoffs, there was a palpable community spirit in the air. I genuinely wished the best for everyone. But of course, I also hoped my cake did well.

The timer on my oven dinged and, nervously, I motioned to a camera that I was about to take out my cake. This was it.

Putting on my oven gloves like I was going into battle, I removed the gooseberry upside-down cake and walked it to the counter. This was what scared me the most: I'd have to be brave...and flip it.

So, of course, this was when the cameras homed in on me. Elspeth and Jonathon joined them, and so I had quite the audience. But at this point I was just thankful that neither of the comedians were there to make me the butt of their jokes. I tried to look relaxed for the cameras, but I knew that I was perspiring at the temples. Argh, how was my cake going to do when I myself was never the right temperature?

Nervously, I ran a flat spatula around the perimeter of the tin to gently coax the sponge from its sides. Next, I took my pretty glass cake stand and held it on top of the tin. Was there a protection spell for upside-down cakes?

"You've got this, Poppy," Gerry said, standing behind Elspeth and for once not clowning. "Take your time."

Easy for him to say—he'd never have to worry about being nervous again. I looked up and caught Elspeth's eye and immediately felt better. I raised the glass to the tin and, holding their sides, turned them in the air. Back on the work-top, I used my flat spatula again and worked the sides, just in case there were any goopy gooseberries in a sticky mood. There was nothing for it—I slowly, I mean, like slow-motion slowly, lifted the tin. And then I shut my eyes. I couldn't bear to see if it was a disaster.

"Yes," Gerry said, sounding as pleased as though he'd scored a triumph. That gave me the courage to open my eyes again.

I'm embarrassed to say that I jumped for joy. All caught on camera, of course. There was no sticking, no collapsing. I peeled away the circular piece of baking parchment and *voila.* A beautiful gooseberry upside-down cake.

"Bravo," said Elspeth, clapping lightly.

"Pretty good, Poppy," Jonathon added.

I beamed.

~

"Two minutes to go, bakers," Jilly called out.

I quickly arranged my mini raspberry meringues around my cake. And I was finished. I couldn't believe I'd managed to pull all that off in the time limit. I stood back and admired my handiwork. So long as the flavors worked, I was actually proud of my cake.

Around me, with a minute to go, there was panic in the air. Amara was slicing peppered strawberries so quickly, I was worried for the tips of her fingers; Hamish hadn't even plated his sponge yet. Maggie had finished her raspberry Victoria Sponge, and Florence was finished, too, and watching everyone just like me. She caught my eye and blew me a kiss. "That looks gorgeous, Pops," she said admiringly. I thanked her and returned the compliment. Her rhubarb concoction smelled and looked divine—pretty in pink.

"Time's up, bakers," Arty called out. "Please bring your fruit cakes to the judging table."

As we all walked over and placed our offering before the judges, I couldn't help but imagine a montage scene of close-up shots of our cakes. They were certainly beautiful to behold. Glossy and full of color. We'd upped our game this week, for sure. Gerry reappeared and mimicked stuffing his face. I tried not to laugh. We were going to have a serious talk very soon. When no one was around to witness it.

Once the cakes were in a row, Jonathon took a step forward.

"Well done, bakers. You've successfully completed your first challenge. And no disasters. Or at least—not yet."

There was some nervous tittering at that. I mean, he couldn't expect us to actually laugh at our worst fears, right?

"First, we're going to cut the cakes in half. This way we can see if anyone has attempted to hide a burned or sunken sponge."

There was a collective gasp, and everyone leaned forward in their chairs. Oooh, that devilish Jonathon. He didn't let us get away with a thing.

"We'll be looking at the color and texture of your sponge to see how proficiently you mixed your ingredients," Elspeth added. "We want to make sure it hasn't been overbeaten or if you've been too heavy-handed with the butter. We want an even texture."

I think I held my breath for the full five minutes it took for Elspeth and Jonathon to eat their way through the table. The usual suspects received praise: Maggie and Florence both with glowing reviews and Amara up there with them. Sadly for Hamish, he didn't quite pull off the parsnip mash-up, with Elspeth positively wrinkling up her delicate nose at the taste. And it was another difficult moment for Evie, who'd crumbled a bit under pressure last week.

Her strawberry shortcake looked perfect, but in this case, beauty was only skin deep. "Your cake is a little soggy, dear," Elspeth said.

"And no one likes a soggy bottom," Arty threw in.

Evie went bright pink and began to turn her rings nervously on her fingers. The poor woman. My heart went out to her.

My cake was last. And by that time, my nerves were stretched to their limit.

As Jonathon raised a forkful to his mouth, I studied every reaction that crossed his face. And boy, I was not disappointed. His blue eyes lit up, his forehead raised in pleasurable surprise as a massive smile spread across his face. He liked it.

AND ELSPETH WAS THE SAME. "My goodness, this is quite delicious. Moist, tart and sweet all at once. And those crispy meringues are perfect with the soft gooseberries. It's a marvel."

I was so happy, I didn't know what to say. Gerry did a little victory dance. I tried not to giggle.

There was a wait, always excruciating, while the judges conferred. And then it happened. They crowned my cake the winner. It was like time had sped up. Everything was spinny and surreal.

Florence and Maggie were by my side, showering me in hugs, and the men clapped me lightly on the back and said what a good job I'd done. Gerry turned cartwheels across the tent.

The only straight thought I had was how much I wanted to tell Susan. Her farm goods had been the real heroes today. I was certain that I had the happy eggs, contented bees and sheltered gooseberries to thank. I'd save her a piece of my cake and take it to her so I could tell her the good news. Just as soon as filming finished.

The cameras hadn't even stopped rolling when one of the cameramen whipped a fork out from his pocket and dug into my cake. "That's fantastic," he said. Jilly smacked his hands away and proceeded to cut my cake into slices for the crew and other contestants to try.

I was floating on air when who did I notice but Sly, watching me from the entrance of the tent. And there was his orange ball his feet. He was as bad as Gerry for distracting me. I hoped he wouldn't try to come in, then noticed one of the crew arrive with some rope and tie him up where he could see us but not interfere. He seemed happy to watch me, as though he knew perfectly well that as soon as I was free, he'd have his ball-throwing slave back.

When the break was called, I made sure to get a piece of my cake, then slipped away and over to the lunch table. I took a roast beef sandwich and, removing the meat, went to Sly. "There you are, my sweet boy," I said. "You eat this up, and later I'll find you a juicy bone." He gobbled up the treat and then nudged the ball with his nose in my direction. He had a completely one-track mind. "Later," I promised him.

I noticed that a few locals had come out to watch the show being filmed. They had to stay behind a barrier, but it was cool being a token celebrity as they snapped photos of the famous tent. I recognized a very pretty girl who was one of the kitchen helpers at the big house. Gerry was trying to look down her shirt, but all he accomplished was making her shiver and button her sweater up. Good.

Eve was there, but I suspected she'd only come out for a bit of fresh air. Beside her was the silver fox who Susan

Bentley had been visiting yesterday afternoon. As I watched, he said something to Eve, and she laughed. They chatted for a few minutes. I was glad that she knew him so I could find out who he was and if Susan Bentley had an interest outside the home.

Honestly, I'd only been here two weekends, and I was already becoming fascinated by the village and its gossip.

The salesman from the pub, Bob Fielding, was also watching. Then he glanced at his watch and turned to take the path to Broomewode Hall. *And good luck to you getting in.* I was about to head back when I saw the horrible gardener, Peter Puddifoot, come stomping over, looking annoyed. But maybe that was his normal expression. I'd never seen him look anything but annoyed.

I immediately went to pet Sly, determined to protect the dog from further violence, but it seemed Mr. Puddifoot wasn't after the dog. He went by the viewers, telling them to move off the lawn and onto the gravel path. He acted like the lawn belonged to him.

Well, if he terrorized the show's onlookers, it meant Sly was safe and I could return to my workstation.

$\mathcal{I}$t was time for the second challenge of the day. Truthfully, I was more in the mood for celebrating in the pub than baking—and I hadn't been looking forward to making madeleines. I didn't get the obsession with these small French sponge cakes. Yes, the fact that they were shaped like a shell was pretty darn cute, but apart from that, I didn't think they were anything special. *And* they were so easy to burn.

We all had to follow Elspeth's classic recipe, and put our own spin on it, and this intensified the pressure. I didn't want to let Elspeth down now, not when the morning had gone so well. But at least this challenge wouldn't take as long as the fruit cakes. I was riding the high of the morning and couldn't wait to be done filming for the day. Celebrating couldn't come soon enough.

Before we began, I wanted my hair and makeup touched up. Okay, I wanted an excuse to let Gina rave about my win. I had to patiently wait for her to finish re-powdering Jonathon's perpetually shiny nose before it was my turn. I was absolutely dying to run through every detail of my win.

The minute she finished, Gina waved me over, manically brandishing a blusher blush.

"Pops! My baking superstar. How lucky I am to have known you since you were a little kid, always licking the bowl when Dad finished making cakes."

I laughed. "I really do have your family to thank for giving me the gift of baking." I grew emotional as I always did when I thought about how important Gina and her family had been in my life. They'd literally saved me, discovering me in a box outside the family's bakery when I was only a few hours old. They'd been part of my life ever since.

She hugged me, then ushered me into her makeup seat. As she re-glossed my lips and tidied up my brows, she told me that the entire crew couldn't stop talking about my cake over lunch.

I grinned. "It's still sinking in, to be honest. After everything that happened last week...well, it's nice to have something to celebrate."

Once Gina had prettified me and got the flour out of the back of my hair (mortifying), the new soundman, Robbie, came over to attach my mic. He said he wasn't long out of college and was extremely happy to have this job. He was chatting away about his new motorcycle, but I was already thinking ahead to madeleines. I discovered that having the winning cake in the morning only made me more anxious not to screw up in the afternoon.

Soon I was back at my station, dutifully weighing out my ingredients according to Elspeth's recipe. Here was the sneaky thing. We got the list of ingredients, but no clues on how to make the madeleines. We were on our own. Sugar, flour, baking powder, butter, two more happy eggs, and a little lemon juice. It looked easy, but I knew that the talent was in the making, the subtleties of how we each manipulated the same ingredients. I had to whisk the eggs and sugar together until they were perfectly frothy, and that was something you could only judge by eye and experience. When this was done, we would leave them to stand for twenty minutes before carefully pouring them into a madeleine tray.

Naturally, we were never allowed to rest. We were each to add a bit of whimsy or slightly different flavors to our madeleines. Since the little cakes originated in France, I decided to use lavender along with the lemon in my mixture. In the twenty minutes the batter rested, I prepared my icing. I was going to pipe a tiny Eiffel Tower of chocolate on each one.

I took a moment to look around the room and see how everyone else was doing. I must have been concentrating harder than I'd thought, because there was some kind of drama happening at the other end of the tent, and I could hear the first gut-wrenching beginnings of a sob. I left my workstation and headed over to the crowd of cameras and both comedians, not that there was anything to joke about. It was Evie. She was crying next to a bowl of spilled batter. It ran all along her workstation and onto the tiled floor. This was pretty much everyone's worst nightmare.

"Don't worry," Maggie was saying. "Just take some deep breaths and you can start again."

"But I don't have time," she wailed. "What's wrong with me? Why do I crack under pressure like this? I make madeleines for my colleagues at the hospital all the time. I can do it in my sleep."

My heart went out to Evie. It was so hard keeping it together when you knew that the cameras were watching your every move. She was using orange juice instead of lemon, and I offered to cut her oranges and redo her juice. Maggie handed her a tissue, and she blew her nose with a loud honk. I hoped for her sake the series producers would edit that out. She took a deep breath and then weighed out some flour again.

"You can do this, Evie," I said, handing her the fresh-squeezed orange juice. "We all believe in you." I gave her my widest smile, and then went to check on my oven temperature. I couldn't afford to make any silly mistakes either. And that's when I spotted Gerry, peering over Evie's shoulder as she remixed her batch.

"Looks like someone's even unluckier than me," he shouted across the room. "Except the worst thing that can happen to her is getting sent home. Not sent to the spirit world."

Oh, Gerry. At least it was getting easier to ignore his commentary. He'd become a bit like an annoying buzzing sound in my ear that I'd gotten used to pretending wasn't there.

The madeleines only needed eight minutes to bake, so I slid them into the oven and wished them well on their journey to golden brown. It was such a ritual, I wondered if I was unconsciously putting a spell on my baking. Magic was forbidden—no way would I disobey that order—but I'd always wished my baking well. Would I have to stop? But how could wishing my baking well make a difference? I laughed to myself before remembering that I was still being filmed. Don't be a doofus, Poppy.

I fussed with my icing, getting the bag perfect so I could pipe my icing onto the little cakes. As I did so, I let my thoughts drift back to Broomewode Hall. I couldn't wait to deliver my gooseberry stash to Katie. This time I was determined to not only make her spill the village gossip but also to help devise a way for me to look at that oil painting in the dining room up close. Whether I liked it or not, getting Katie on my side was going to involve a bit of truth-telling. If I could get her to feel a little more sorry for me, poor orphaned Poppy, left in an apple crate, then maybe she'd be more willing to help.

When the eight minutes were up, I removed my madeleines from the oven. They looked perfect, golden brown and with a nice, dense, cakey look to them. Phew.

I let them cool on a rack while I got my plate ready.

"You have two minutes left, bakers," Arty called out.

I jumped in my skin. What? Two minutes? How had I lost track of time?

Frantically, I began to pipe Eiffel Towers. Until you have piped a thin stream of chocolate icing onto a barely-cooled madeleine, with a clock ticking down, and the knowledge that millions of people will one day be watching you, you don't know pressure.

What had I been thinking? I should have gone for sprigs of lavender, or even icing meant to mimic lavender. But the Eiffel Tower? It was fiendishly difficult, and the icing wouldn't go on straight, as my hands were slick with nerves.

With thirty seconds to go, I chose the best-looking eight from the dozen I'd baked. Most of them looked more like the

Hindenburg than the Eiffel Tower, but there was nothing I could do but carefully arrange them on a blue ceramic plate. When the clanger went, I breathed out a sigh of relief and then walked back over to the judging table. All I could do now was wait and hope I'd done enough to secure my entry to next week's round.

I took a look at the array of madeleines. Although I'd watched the show so many times at home, I was still surprised at how different everyone's baking looked even though we'd all followed the same recipe. Some were a deeper color, some a little...puffier. I didn't fancy those. The decorations ranged from simple—Maggie had merely sifted icing sugar onto hers, going for a classic look—to elaborate. Florence had used almond essence and dipped the edges of her cakes into dark chocolate and slivers of almond. They looked elegant and perfect.

Mine looked absolutely amateur by comparison. I also didn't feel as attached to my batch as I had to my cake. I'd poured so much of my personality into that little gooseberry guy that making another person's recipe meant that the whole challenge felt, well, less personal. Even still, I held my breath again as Elspeth and Jonathon whipped through the tasting. What if I *had* made a silly mistake? Did I leave out the sugar? Could I?

When it was my turn to be judged, Jonathon said, "You made a bit of mess with your icing, Poppy," and Elspeth nodded. Still, when they tasted my little cakes, Jonathon complimented the airy texture, and Elspeth said it had a nice crumb to it. The rest of the judging went by in a blur. Amara was crowned the winner of the round, having painted each of her cakes with food coloring, so they looked like tiny, perfect impressionist paintings. Maggie was second, because the judges said she'd gone with simplicity in her decorating but perfection in her batter. Euan was third. Maybe because she'd started again from scratch, poor Evie hadn't managed to bake her madeleines for long enough, and they were wet in the middle.

"Not enough flour in these, Evie," Jonathon said, shaking his head.

"I think you mean they're undercooked, Jonathon," Elspeth said, shooting him a quick glare. They had to film that little critique again, with Jonathon correcting himself and poor Evie trying to stifle a sob. Everyone crowded round to comfort her. "I know exactly how to make them. I don't know what's wrong with me," she whispered.

Evie was second from last. Gaurav had overbaked his, so the judges complained that madeleines weren't meant to crunch. "It's not a cookie, mate," Jonathon reminded him.

I ended up fifth. Florence sixth. Seemed she went too heavy on the almond essence and had overbaked her pretty cakes.

Although I hadn't made the top three, I tried not to feel too badly about it. Maybe I'd just run out of steam after my win this morning. Florence hadn't made the top three either. She pouted and looked upset as filming ended and the crew dug into the plates of madeleines. I honestly didn't know where they managed to put all that cake.

"Don't worry, Florence," I said, taking her hand. "Tomorrow we'll both claw our way back into the top three."

Her eyes brimmed with tears. "What if I don't do well tomorrow, either? I could be sent home." It was a bit dramatic, but that was Florence. Film star to the core, married to the drama. But, she was right. Any of us could end up going home.

For now, I was just glad to take off my butter-smeared apron, and with filming finally over for the day, it was the perfect time to visit Susan, tell her the good news about my big win, and give Sly that juicy bone I'd promised him. I'd managed to save a slice of the gooseberry cake for Susan and only hoped she'd like it as much as the judges had.

As soon as I stepped foot out of the tent, there was Sly, tail wagging, orange ball at his feet. I looked down at myself and realized that this gooey, slobbered-on dog's ball exactly matched the color of my shirt.

All the viewers had gone home for the day. No doubt they had lives to live, and the afternoon had grown chilly. Peter Puddifoot came stomping down the path from the manor house. I bet he'd been up there complaining about people daring to stand on "his" lawn. I wondered why the Champneys put up with him. Or were they stuck with him? Perhaps he was Grade II listed like that ancient and dangerous tower?

"Sly," I said, bending to give him a stroke. "What are you still doing here? Susan is going to be worried. Or she'll think I'm a dog-napper." Come to think of it, if I ever had a dog, I'd want one exactly like Sly.

He wagged his tail in response and nosed his ball toward my feet.

"I've got something even more exciting than your ball," I promised him, gripping the bag with the bone. He sniffed greedily, then grabbed the ball between his strong teeth and dropped it at my feet. Play before food, he seemed to be saying.

"Come on, then, you pesky thing." I threw the ball as far

as I could and began walking in the direction of Broomewode Farm.

The sun was making its way behind the trees now, and Broomewode Hall was cast in a marigold glow. Later, I'd visit Katie and bring her my gooseberry haul from Susan's plot. I pictured the joy on her face when she saw them, knowing that she could make the Champneys their jam without having to pick one-handed. I did hope her broken arm was healing well. Once inside the house, I'd have to find a cunning way to get into the dining room and examine the painting of the woman in my baby blanket up close. But the details of that particular scheme could be worked out later. Today was about celebrating and recharging before the final challenge.

I slipped on my cardigan and buttoned it up. It was amazing how cool early evening could get at this time of year, but I definitely still felt that warm glow inside from my win this morning. I took out my phone to call my parents and tell them all about it. It'd been ages since we last spoke, mostly because I didn't want to worry them with the drama of the last week. But now—finally—I had good news.

My dad answered the phone. "Poppy. We've been waiting for your call. How's it going? Is our girl the star baker? You know, whatever happens, you're always the star baker to your mother and I."

I loved how supportive they were. Whatever my origins, I had to remember how lucky I'd been to end up with Agatha and Leland as my parents. And whatever I learned of my heritage, they would always be my mom and dad.

"Let me put you on speakerphone. Mom's right here."

There was a shuffle and then my mom's voice came on the

line, flooding me with the same kind of warmth that lately only Elspeth had been able to provide. It was so nice to hear her. I gave them both a blow-by-blow account of my gooseberry win, and they were thrilled. A little too thrilled. "We're so proud of you. When you didn't call after last week, we thought maybe you'd been voted off and didn't want to talk about it."

I felt immediately guilty. It wasn't my performance on the show I'd wanted to keep from them but the horror of a murder in the tent. However, I could tell them all about that when filming was over. Living in the south of France, they were unlikely to hear there'd been a murder. Someone, somewhere must have some pull, for there'd been surprisingly little coverage of the baking show crime. "You have to promise me that you won't tell anyone. You have to keep this under wraps until the show airs, okay? I could get in serious trouble."

"Do you want us to sign a non-disclosure agreement?" Dad was joking, but I really shouldn't have told them about my baking win. However, I knew I could trust them. They'd be able to enjoy my win and talk about it when they were on their own. I couldn't imagine not telling them.

"We promise, Pops," my mom said. "But on one condition: you promise to come visit once filming is done. It's been far too long. We miss you."

I made my promise. I missed them, too.

By the time I'd hung up, Sly and I had reached the farmhouse, its sprawling shape silhouetted against the setting sun. The Range Rover was out front, and lights were on inside, but when I rang the doorbell, there was no answer.

"That's odd," I said to Sly. "Maybe they're out back and can't hear me?"

But Sly dropped his ball and raised his nose in the air, sniffing. I saw the ruff on his neck rise, and he began whining.

"What is it, hey? What are you trying to tell me?"

Sly kept sniffing the air and suddenly began to bark. Then he nudged me, ran off and turned, so clearly waiting for me to follow. So, dutifully, I did.

I didn't want to be snooping on near-strangers' property, but Sly wasn't the goofy playmate obsessed with his ball. He'd transformed into working dog mode, and he was definitely trying to herd me somewhere he thought I should go.

As we turned and approached the left side of the house, I could see the outline of the chicken coop and Susan's beehives in the distance. Sly bolted toward them. What was he going to do? Herd the bees?

He began to run and, again driven by an impulse I didn't fully understand, I broke into a run and followed.

For the second time that week, I wished I'd spent a little more time on the treadmill and less time baking. I made a mental promise to hit the gym this week. Clearly, I had to be prepared for anything. Like spontaneous dog-running.

But as we got closer to the beehives, I saw exactly why Sly was sprinting. Instead of neat rows of hives, one had toppled over, and a swarming, buzzing, great mass of bees had formed into an angry ball. Sly turned back to me and barked again. I swear he was telling me to get a move on.

And that's when I saw the Bentleys.

Arnold was on the ground, flat on his back, and Susan was on her knees beside him, frantically searching his pockets. There were bees zooming all around the pair, but Susan didn't seem to notice.

For a man with a bee allergy, Arnold Bentley couldn't be in a more dangerous place.

"Susan?" I called out. "What can I do?"

She looked up at me, horror-stricken, her red cheeks now deathly pale.

"His EpiPen!" she shouted. "I can't find it, and I can't leave him. There's one in the kitchen."

Time slowed right down. I looked at her, then at the fallen beehive, and back to the body of her husband, which was twitching now with an alarming motion.

I sprang into action. No way was someone else going to die this week. Not on my watch, and not if Sly had anything to do with it, either. I turned and began to run back, not caring that my lungs were bursting and I had a stitch in my side. Sly was a black and white blur as he ran past and ahead of me, toward an open side door. Sly barked twice, and I took that as confirmation it was the right entrance. I ran like a maniac, almost tripping over a stray vine, and into the farmhouse.

Once inside, I couldn't figure out where the kitchen was. I looked about the flagstone hallway in a fluster, stepping over abandoned gumboots and almost clattering into an umbrella stand. An old oak table held a newspaper and a half-drunk mug of coffee. Bookcases lined the hallway. I needed to find the kitchen, find the EpiPen.

Sly barked and ran to the other end of the hall and stopped at a small ottoman, illuminated by a table lamp with a striped cream lampshade. I dashed over and found a round ceramic dish with two pairs of keys and an EpiPen nestled inside. Yes! "Good boy," I panted, grabbing the pen.

I ran back to the Bentleys.

Susan had her head on her husband's chest and was sobbing.

"I've got it! I've got it!" I cried out, jubilant, thrusting the pen in Susan's face.

She lifted her head wearily. Her eyes were red and streaming. In a tiny voice, she said, "It's too late. He's...he's dead."

CHAPTER 8

*I*t was night by the time DI Hembly and Sgt. Lane
knocked on Susan's door. I'd watched the color of
the sky change through the latticed windows—dusky pink to
rich orange until the horizon was shot through with inky
black. The ambulance had come and gone, and Sly lay at
Susan's feet, quietly guarding her. Comforting her.

"I can't understand it," she kept saying. "Why would he go
near the hives? And without his pen? It doesn't make sense."
It was like a loop that kept going round and round as she
repeated the words.

We were both stunned, and I had no idea how to comfort
this poor grieving woman. Widow, now. Anything I tried to
say sounded corny or stuck in my throat.

It was me who'd called 999, then waited for the ambulance. Sadly, there was nothing the paramedics could do.
Susan had been right. Her husband was dead.

She was in shock, and I couldn't leave her, so I made mugs
of tea, which lay untouched, steam floating up. For my part, I

couldn't believe that this was the second dead body I'd come across in two weeks. Was I a bad penny? Had I brought the bad juju to Broomewode Hall?

When the doorbell rang, Susan didn't look up from the third mug of tea I'd made her, so I went to answer the door myself, my heart heavy. Sly barked and ran ahead of me to the door. It seemed I was part of his flock now, and he was a faithful guard dog.

In normal circumstances, opening the door to two police officers would bring on a bout of panic, but after the weird goings-on since I'd first arrived here, the sight of DI Hembly and Sgt. Lane was a strange comfort. They dealt with death every day. They'd know what to do.

Their features were already familiar to me: Sgt. Lane's long Roman nose, deep-set brown eyes, full mouth, and clean-shaven cheeks inset with dimples that I suspected he despised. He must have been to the barbers since last week, because his flop of dark brown hair was shorter. As he gave me a small smile, his dimples transformed his serious face. DI Hembly's gray buzz cut was perfectly crisp, and his square jaw remained serious. He wore a blazer over his white shirt and navy trousers, and his brown shoes were gleaming.

"Poppy," DI Hembly said, somewhat taken aback, "I didn't expect to find you here."

And how I wished I wasn't. I ushered the two officers inside the cottage. "I had come to visit Susan when her husband, Arnold, sadly passed away."

"I see," DI Hembly said in that soft, patient voice of his, which reminded me of my dad.

"Wrong place, wrong time," I said, shaking my head.

"Is Susan Bentley inside?" DI Hembly continued.

I nodded and led them both into the kitchen. Susan was still staring at her mug of tea. She raised her head as we walked in, and DI Hembly introduced both the officers.

"Mrs. Bentley," Sgt. Lane said, "I'm so sorry for your loss."

Susan looked blankly at the officers and gave a short nod. Her eyes were red from crying, and her cheeks were streaked with fresh tears. The strong, solid woman I'd met on Friday had all but disappeared. "Police," she said, as though she couldn't believe they had any reason to be in her farmhouse kitchen, and, indeed, the two looked out of place among the big pots, the shelves of honey and the Aga stove.

"I'm afraid the police have to investigate all sudden deaths so that they can make a report to the coroner. There will have to be an inquest," DI Hembly continued. "May we sit down and ask a few simple questions? We'll get this over with as quickly as we can."

"Of course, of course," Susan mumbled. She picked up her teaspoon and heaped some sugar into her tea. One scoop, then two, then three. She stopped suddenly. "Oh. I don't think I meant to do that."

"I'll put the kettle back on," I offered. I guessed tea-making would have to be my superpower today.

As the kettle boiled, I stared out of the farmhouse's window, vaguely listening. I couldn't stop thinking about my own family, the one I knew and loved, and the other one I'd yet to find. Seeing someone lose their husband really brought home how much I had to cherish the people around me. I set down four more mugs of tea on the scrubbed pine kitchen table, and this time Susan finally took a sip. "I don't under-stand how it happened." And then she began to cry again.

"Take your time," DI Hembly said. "But could you talk me through what happened to your husband?"

Susan shook as she cried, and I reached out and held her hand, giving it a little squeeze. If only Elspeth was here, she'd know what to say and do. I wished that I could make Susan feel calm, the way that Elspeth did for me. I squeezed her hand tighter and concentrated on breathing evenly, trying to communicate with her. To my surprise, her breathing began to slow.

"I'm right here with you, Susan," I said quietly.

"In your own time," Sgt. Lane said, softening his voice. "There's no rush."

Susan took another sip of her tea and then began talking. "I was—I was out on the tractor, up over the hill, ploughing some of our land. I do a lot of the manual stuff here, you see, because my husband isn't...wasn't in great health. And he has to be very careful because he's allergic to bee stings. So I don't understand what he was doing there. Why would he go there? And without his EpiPen? He carried it everywhere."

"Go where, Mrs. Bentley?" Sgt. Lane asked. He had his notebook open.

"The beehives. He'd never go near them. Never. One of them was knocked over, you see, but why would he try and sort it out? He'd leave it to me."

"Is that where you found him? The beehives? How many exactly are there?"

Susan took another sip of tea. "Yes. I came back from the fields. I have to pass the beehives to get back to the house—there are four hives—and I saw in the distance that a hive had been knocked over. I was only thinking of the bees. It wasn't until I got closer that I saw him. On the ground." In mine, her hand began to tremble. "He couldn't breathe. He was gasping. Trying to speak, but all I could hear was him wheezing."

Sgt. Lane looked up from his notepad. "So, let me get this right. Your husband was lying by the fallen hive? Even though he's allergic to bees?"

"Yes. It makes no sense for him to have been there. He usually only traveled between the front door and his car. Sometimes he'd sit out on the back patio, but rarely. He was so frightened of being stung, you see. And what's more, he didn't have his EpiPen with him. And he never leaves the house without it. Never. Even *in* the house, there's always one in his pocket."

As Susan spoke, Sgt. Lane kept up his rapid note-taking in his small black book. I sipped my sweet tea, wishing I could use my witchy powers and turn back time for Susan. I also wished for a vanishing spell. I wanted to be a million miles away from this table, back with my mum and dad in our old kitchen, maybe eating my dad's famous pancakes covered in blueberries and maple syrup.

"Has a hive ever toppled over like that before?" DI Hembly asked.

"No, not in the four years we've been here at the farm. I look after those bees like they're family. Everything is well maintained. I can't imagine what happened for the hive to be knocked over like that." She gave a gasp. "I should have let him give the bees away. He wanted to, you know, but I love beekeeping. I love gathering the honey and the wax for candles. Bees are peaceful creatures. They only sting if provoked. So long as Arnold left them alone, I was certain he'd be safe." Her voice choked again with tears. "But he wasn't. This is all my fault." She looked at the two officers. "I killed my husband."

The two officers exchanged a glance. Had this woman just admitted to murder?

"Why do you say that, Mrs. Bentley?"

"Because I argued against him giving the bees away. I just told you. If I'd been more supportive, they'd be gone by now. Reg would have them, and my husband would be alive."

Except that I recalled Peter Puddifoot's shouted words to Arnold Bentley about moving bees. I had no idea if he'd been telling the truth, but a woman who'd worked with the insects for four years must know. For the first time I spoke, hoping the cops wouldn't mind me interfering. "But they might have come back, mightn't they? Don't bees need to be moved a long way if they're not to return to their former home?"

She turned to me, and her green eyes looked eager. As though she'd forgotten this fact. "Yes. Exactly. Reg only lives a mile away. It's not far enough."

"Reg?" Sergeant Lane asked her.

"Reginald McMahan. He said in the pub one night that he wanted to start hives. He was only looking for advice, but Arnold immediately told him he could have our hives and welcome to them. I wasn't very happy, as you can imagine, but I would have gone along with it except that Reg—that Mr. McMahon—only lives on the other side of the village. In the old blacksmith's cottage. Bees can be moved a couple of feet and still get back to the hive, or you can move them miles away and they'll adjust. But if they're close enough to the original site, they'll return there instead of the new hives.

Frankly, I thought it would be more dangerous for Arnold and probably deadly for the bees."

She looked around, stricken. "Did I put the welfare of my bees ahead of my own husband?"

No one answered. I was certain she'd done the best she could and wasn't responsible for her husband's tragic end, but she was currently being questioned by police, and it wasn't my place to keep butting in. I buttoned my lip, vowing to talk to her quietly after they'd left and reassure her as best I could. Susan Bentley hadn't caused her husband's death. I was sure of it.

However, she might have hurt him in other ways. I now had a name for the silver fox who lived at the old blacksmith's cottage in Broomewode Village. Reginald McMahan. She'd slipped and called him Reg, which suggested they were friendly, but how friendly exactly?

"When did you first notice the hive was on the ground?" DI Hembly asked.

"They were fine this morning. I can see them when I go to let the chickens out. I fetched eggs, checked on the hens, and returned. That was about nine this morning." She was sounding more together now that she was focused on remembering.

"And when did you first notice the hive was on its side?"

"Not until late this afternoon. I could see something was wrong. The bees were obviously disturbed, but it wasn't until I got closer that I noticed one of the hives was on its side. And Arnold was on the ground."

"Might the hive have been pushed over?"

Susan looked at the two officers and then at me. "That's what I've been sitting here thinking. I can't figure out any other reason why it'd be on the ground like that. Bored teenagers, not realizing that a prank like that could be deadly. A stray animal, maybe. I wondered about weather, but it hasn't even been windy."

How many bored teenagers were there in Broomewode? I hadn't seen a single one. I also couldn't imagine an animal knocking over the hive. In the Pacific Northwest where bears still roamed and loved honey, then sure. But out here?

"Mrs. Bentley, did your husband have any enemies?" DI Hembly asked. At the question, I stopped thinking about bears and my attention sharpened.

"Enemies? Are you trying to say that someone might have done this on purpose?"

"We're just trying to get a clearer picture, that's all. Did he?"

Susan hesitated, patting Sly's head absentmindedly. "Not here. Or not that I know of."

Ha. What about Peter Puddifoot? With the angry face and the animal cruelty?

"Arnold worked in the finance district in London. It wasn't an easy environment, and the stress got to him." She paused. "He ran his own investment fund, you see. He was never one who followed trends and did what every other fund manager did. He was daring, and he made many of his clients rich." She stopped to bite her lip. "But he took risks. That's why the returns were so high. When his technique stopped working, it went badly wrong, and he crumbled under the pressure. I think there may have been a few people he upset in the process. Money lost and all that. But not so badly that they'd do something unspeakable. *We* were the ones who lost a lot of money. Everything. I mean, we drive that old Land Rover now. The Porsche and the Mayfair home are long gone. We had to sell our home in Saint-Tropez."

I appreciated that these were real tragedies to Susan Bentley, but in truth, I felt like playing the world's tiniest violin.

"We moved here because Lord Frome was an old client of Arnold's and gave us a good deal on the property." She smiled sadly. "Arnold would have hated me to tell you that. He was so proud. We always pretended we were well-off, when the truth was, we were barely making ends meet."

DI Hembly nodded. "Thank you. That's very helpful to know." He paused. "Apart from Lord Frome, was he in contact with other old clients?"

She shook her head. "I don't think so. Our friends and Arnold's colleagues mainly deserted us at the first hint of trouble. I try to be forgiving, but it hasn't been easy."

"What about disgruntled clients? Was anyone harassing your husband?"

"It all happened more than five years ago. There were lawsuits." She shuddered. "It was awful."

"We'll need names of all the complainants."

"Of course. I'll put you on to our lawyer, but I really think—"

"Just covering all possibilities, Mrs. Bentley. We like to be thorough."

Sgt. Lane jotted down the name of Arnold's old firm, the lawyer's name and a few of his closest colleagues. The names Susan could remember.

"I think that's all for the time being, Mrs. Bentley," DI Hembly said. He handed her his card and asked that she call him if she thought of anything else that could be useful.

"We'll walk around your property now. We'll need to see the hives."

She looked up, alarmed. "But it's dark. And you mustn't go too close. They're still very upset. I wouldn't want you to get stung." Then she looked from one to the other. "You're not allergic, are you?"

"We won't go too close," DI Hembly said in his soothing tone. "We'll come back in the daylight to examine the area properly."

They stood from the table, and I rose with them. DI Hembly's phone buzzed, and he frowned at whatever message had just come through. "Poppy, if you could wait a few minutes, Sgt. Lane here will walk back with you to the inn. I'm needed back at the station. He'll just ask you a couple of questions about what you saw when you arrived at the scene this evening. Nothing to worry about, you understand."

I swallowed. Even though I knew that I wasn't under suspicion, I still felt awkward being once more on the scene of a death. I picked up my tote bag and remembered Sly's bone wrapped up inside. And the cake. It seemed a hundred years had gone by since I won the challenge. "Will you be okay?" I asked Susan. "I can stay here with you."

She thanked me but shook her head. "Reg is on his way. He'll help me right the hive. I must get the bees resettled." I was shocked that "Reg" was rushing to her side when poor Arnold was barely cold. Perhaps she read my expression, for she added, "And I've sisters in the area. They'll help me."

The police officers shared a glance. "We'd prefer you leave the area exactly as it is, Mrs. Bentley. Until it's light and we can have a proper look."

I could tell she was about to argue, and then she slumped back into her chair. "Yes. Of course."

I told her about Sly's bone and put it in the fridge for later. On the counter beside the stove was an EpiPen. If only Arnold Bentley hadn't forgotten his pen, he'd be alive at this moment. I debated with myself, then put the slice of gooseberry cake on the table. "Thanks to your bees and hens and the gooseberries, my cake won the challenge this morning."

Her pale face brightened. "That's wonderful. I'll be sure and eat this when I feel up to it."

"Please do. You must try to eat something. Keep your strength up." I had so little experience with grieving widows. I wished my mother were here, or Elspeth or an older woman who would know what to say. I was repeating pat phrases I'd probably heard on TV or read in books.

When Sgt. Lane and DI Hembly returned from the hives, I hugged Susan goodbye and gave her my phone number, urging her to call whenever she wanted. Then I bent down and hugged Sly. I knew he'd watch over her tonight.

DI Hembly shook my hand with his firm grip and then got into his car.

Sgt. Lane and I began to walk back to the inn, gravel crunching underfoot. The moon was rising now and so perfectly round, it must be full. In the silvery light, the flowers and plants that had looked so delightful earlier now looked ghostly and unnerving. I shuddered.

"Well, Poppy," Sgt. Lane said. "You've certainly been through a lot in the last couple of weeks. How do you know the Bentleys?" And I realized that he was definitely still on duty. He might be walking me home, but I suspected he was going to gently interrogate me on the way.

I explained about Sly, how he'd run off on Friday and I'd returned him, and then Susan and I got talking and I'd told her I was a contestant on the baking contest. "She let me pick gooseberries on her land and gave me farm eggs and honey from her bees." I stopped at the mention of bees. I had to gather myself before telling him that I'd been returning her dog again and bringing her a slice of the cake I'd made with her produce. I was tempted to tell him about my win but restrained myself.

I could see the old chapel tower lit by moonlight, and I toyed with the idea of telling Sgt. Lane about my near-miss with a rocky end. Maybe it was a coincidence and he'd think I was as much a drama queen as Florence, but I decided to tell him anyway.

"Something else happened yesterday." I stopped and pointed at the tower. "I don't know if this is relevant or not, but gooseberries grow at the base of the tower, and Susan told me that's where the cook at Broomewode Hall, Katie, goes to pick the berries to make jam for the Champneys." *So not relevant. Pull yourself together.* "Anyway, while I was picking berries yesterday, a massive slab of stone fell from the tower and almost flattened me. I mean, I was inches from where it crashed down. I could have been killed." I stopped again, shaking at the memory.

He turned to stare down at me. "How close did it come to hitting you?"

"If the dog hadn't started barking and herded me away, I think I'd be dead." Did he think I was exaggerating? Hard to tell. "Strangely, I'm kind of getting used to weird things happening around here."

"You've been hearing the rumors about the energy vortex,

no doubt." From his tone, I guessed he wasn't a big believer. No doubt he didn't believe in witches, either. "Can you show me where the stone fell?"

Sgt. Lane pulled a flashlight from his pocket and lit the way as I walked us along the path to the tower. I was pleased to see that Benedict, or someone, had put rope around the area and a large sign saying "Danger. Keep off."

Sgt. Lane swung his flashlight around the area. The slab of stone was on the ground, unmoved since it had almost pulverized me.

"You're right. That would have killed you." I felt he could have sounded more shocked. Or at least sympathetic.

"I thought it was an accident, but after what happened this evening, I'm not so sure. It doesn't add up. I met Arnold, only briefly, but long enough to see that he was a cautious man. He was too terrified to come and look at what had happened to the tower for fear of bees. So why would the same man go running toward the beehives, without his EpiPen, and accidentally knock one over? Or if it had already been knocked over, he'd have run in the opposite direction. Not toward the hive. The bees were buzzing all around him. It was an awful sight."

I took a breath in and then told him about the fight I'd overheard between Peter Puddifoot and Arnold Bentley. "I don't know if it's relevant, but when you asked Susan Bentley earlier whether her husband had any enemies, the gardener was the first person who came to mind."

We turned from the tower and back onto the main path. When we came out of the woods and onto the lawns of Broomewode, the inn was silhouetted against the moon, its windows shining with warm yellow light. It looked safe and warm and comfortable. Exactly where I wanted to be.

Sgt. Lane was very quiet, and he looked to be deep in thought. Finally, he said, "You do know what you're suggesting, Poppy?"

I blew out a breath. "Yes. I'm suggesting Arnold Bentley was murdered."

CHAPTER 9

*W*e arrived back at the inn, and Sgt. Lane lingered at the door. The glow of the orange lamp above the entrance tinted his face gold. Those dimples got me every time. He really was a cutie. I stood waiting, somehow knowing that he wanted to say something but was holding back.

"What?" I asked. He hadn't said a word since I'd cried foul play regarding Arnold Bentley's death. "Do you think I'm being hysterical?"

He laid a gentle hand on my shoulder. "We don't know what killed Arnold Bentley yet, but you should be careful. Stay with your group. No wandering at night in the dark."

I smiled, feeling that his interest in my safety wasn't completely professional. Although I knew by now that people weren't always what they seemed (Gordon the murdering sound guy for one). But I had a good feeling about Adam Lane. Maybe it was time to trust my intuition a bit more and place my trust in him, too. Although some of my secrets would have to stay secret. I mean buried right down.

Deep down. I didn't think he could handle a ghost-seeing water witch right now on top of a second murder case.

I promised Sgt. Lane that I'd keep myself safe. He seemed relieved. I made a mental note not to talk to Gateau in front of him and definitely not to react to Gerry's antics if he was around, and then we parted ways. I felt grateful knowing that people like DI Hembly and Sgt. Lane were out there, protecting the community. That fact, and the amethyst around my neck, would hopefully help me get some sleep tonight. Because, murder or no murder, I had the final baking challenge in the morning.

INSIDE THE PUB, the rest of the bakers had mostly dispersed. It wasn't late, only nine p.m., but I figured they were in their rooms, getting ready to bake tomorrow. And that's what I should be doing, too, though the trauma of witnessing a man's death had pretty much dimmed my enthusiasm for baking.

I felt like I'd done several rounds in a boxing ring today, from my highest high, winning the cake challenge, to my lowest low, finding poor Arnold Bentley. I desperately wanted a good meal and a large glass of red wine but wasn't sure I could face anyone who might be left in the pub. I definitely didn't have it in me to make polite conversation about the best temperature for cooking fudge or whatever baking topic was top of the list tonight. Not after what I'd seen this evening.

Besides, I was pretty sure that Gateau would be waiting for me, luxuriating on my bed, and I needed her comfort.

The drama of the evening's events had finally caught up to me, and I felt like someone had drained the life right out of me. I wondered if I could have food sent up to my room. This place didn't have a room service menu, but I bet if Eve was around she'd be willing to send up a tray.

I began to climb the stairs when I heard my name bellowed from the dining room. I winced. It was undeniably Florence's musical voice, and I was busted. I retraced my steps and entered the pub. It smelt of a rich meat stew, and the red tapered candles were flickering on the oak tables. A fire crackled merrily in the grated fireplace, and the whole setup looked so inviting, I almost melted into the chair that Hamish pulled out for me. I joined him, Florence, and Gaurav, who were polishing off a bottle of wine. I felt safe here and among friends. Maybe I didn't want to be on my own after all.

"Where have you been, Pops?" Florence asked, pouting and pouring me a glass of wine. "We wanted to celebrate you and your win today. You always seem to be running off, doing errands, instead of spending time with your friends." I could barely muster a smile, but she was right. I *was* always disappearing from the group, and every time I did, something bad happened.

Florence might be too self-involved to see what was under her nose, but Hamish was a police officer, and I'd found he didn't miss much. He poured me a glass of water from the jug in the middle of the table and handed it to me.

"Are you okay?" Hamish asked, sounding very nasal. "You don't look flushed with victory. In fact, you're very pale. You haven't caught my cold, have you?"

I didn't reply. I took a long drink of the water.

He looked at me again, and then his eyes opened wide. "I've seen that expression on you before." He paused. "I'm drinking a hot whiskey for this cold. It's got plenty of honey in it. Maybe you should have one too. And something to eat?"

I shuddered at the mention of honey. "The wine is fine."

"And you must eat something," Florence insisted.

"Maybe some soup." I couldn't fancy anything heavy. Florence went up to the bar to order for me. She returned and told me that a bowl of minestrone soup was on the way. She might not be very observant, but once she'd been alerted that I was pale, she was a good friend.

"Now, spill whatever it is that's happened," she said. "You're scaring me. Did they decide you didn't win your baking challenge after all?"

I shook my head.

"Something worse? They made a mistake and decided to send you home instead?"

It was so ridiculous, I laughed. "No. Nothing to do with baking."

She put a hand to her chest, her dark nails as dramatic as her fears. "Thank goodness."

I took a long sip of the red wine. I looked at each of their expectant faces and didn't want to ruin the fun of the weekend by telling them someone else had died on the grounds. But in a small village like this, word would soon spread.

So I breathed deeply and told them everything, right from the beginning. How I'd returned Sly, the gooseberry picking, the gifted happy chickens' eggs and contented bees' honey, and that I'd been on my way to tell Susan the good news of my win when I found her and her husband on the ground beside a toppled beehive. I took a breath. "And he was allergic. Deathly allergic. Of course, the bees were homeless and angry, and he was stung. And now he's—"

"Dead?" Florence cried. "Holy mother of God. What craziness is happening at Broomewode?"

Hamish sneezed. "Poor guy. What a way to go. You worry about being allergic to bee stings, and then BAM: worst fear realized."

Guarav was quiet, but his eyes gleamed. I couldn't tell if it was the red wine or the drama of my news. His mind was obviously whirring. He took another sip of his wine and said, "Surely a man allergic to bees would have an EpiPen on him? Like at all times? Especially if his zany wife kept bloomin' bees on their land?"

I nodded sadly. "That's the thing. Arnold did always keep an EpiPen in his pocket. And he never went anywhere near the beehives." I looked at Hamish. "It *was* his worst fear. Susan said he often had two EpiPens on him. So what he was doing by the beehives and leaving the house without a pen... It doesn't make sense."

Hamish was shaking his head. "Nope. This doesn't add up at all. I hate to say it, but it sounds a lot like—"

"Don't say murder," Florence implored him.

Gaurav was gobsmacked. "Come on," he said, disbelief spreading across his face. "I know last weekend was a shocker, and we're all kind of recovering from what happened to Gerry, but we can't go jumping to wild conclusions. It's an unfortunate accident, that's all."

Wow. I guess it took a bee-related death to bring shy Gaurav out of his shell.

Hamish looked thoughtful. "I think I have to agree with

Gaurav here. I've never worked with the homicide department, but years of being a beat police officer tells me there's just no motive here. Why would anyone murder a retiree tucked away in a tiny village in Somerset?"

It was a good question. My bowl of soup arrived. It smelled fragrant and herby, and the curls of pasta floating on top looked delicious. I quickly buttered a warm, crusty chunk of baguette and tucked in. I was famished again. What would it take to truly throw off my appetite? The apocalypse? Probably not even then—I had images of me chowing down on a cheeseburger while the world went up in flames and the cockroaches reigned supreme.

"If there's one thing Gordon taught us, it's that first impressions can sometimes count for nothing," Florence said. "Just think about it: this time last week we were breaking bread with a homicidal manic. We *welcomed* him into our fold."

"True," Hamish said, shaking his head. "I even bought the rotter a beer. Maybe my instincts aren't what they used to be."

I looked up from my soup. "Don't say that, Hamish. None of us could have predicted how Gordon would turn out."

"So what I'm saying is," Florence said, steering the conversation back to her musings, "maybe this Arnold Bentley wasn't who he appeared to be, either."

I said nothing. I agreed wholeheartedly, but I really didn't want to be the one who led my fellow bakers away from the food processor toward conspiracy theories. I took another bite of my baguette.

"We could look him up on the internet," Florence said, whipping out her phone. "What was his full name?"

"Arnold Bentley, no idea of his middle name." I wondered

how much I could share from overhearing a police questioning and then remembered that Susan had told me of her husband's former profession before he'd died. I wouldn't reveal anything she'd said to the police, but I didn't feel like I was breaking rules to share that he'd been in London and worked in investments.

"Good," Hamish said, scooting next to Florence to stare at her screen. The moonlight shone through the pub's window and spilled onto Florence's hands as her long, polished nails tapped across the phone.

I shook my head and kept eating. I'd had a mini debate with myself as to whether to tell the group about my near miss with the falling stone. Now I was especially glad I hadn't. The last thing I wanted was to stir up any more fuss and amateur detective work. Although Hamish was no amateur. I kept forgetting that his real-life job was on the force. To me he was a brilliant baker with a flair for fondant icing. I spooned the last of my soup and turned my attention back to the internet stalking I'd accidentally encouraged. Way to go, Pops.

"Hmmm," Florence said, frowning. "A Facebook profile page of someone in Florida." She swiped a few times. "Ooh, this looks promising. It's a business networking site. You said he was in finance, right?"

I nodded reluctantly.

"Oh. This Arnold Bentley is a thirty-two-year-old architect." Florence sighed. Gaurav had returned to his silent self, but he was watching Florence's search the way I watched my dad trying to text. With amusement. Like me, he seemed to be having some internal battle. But I guess one side overcame the other because he said, "You won't get very far like that. Let me have a look."

"You're in biochemistry," Florence replied. "What do you know about internet research? I have to do *a lot* of background work when I'm preparing a character."

"I'm pretty good with computers." Gaurav stood. "Gimme a sec. I'll be back with my laptop."

I took another sip of my wine. Florence and Hamish tried to prod me for more details. If these three wanted to find out what really happened to Arnold Bentley, then who was I to stop them? I'd brought them the information, and now I was going to have to deal with the consequences.

I described Arnold in detail, from the sweep of gray hair, elegantly combed away from his high forehead, down to the navy cashmere sweater he'd been wearing when I first saw him in the pub and flannel trousers. "And he had these really polished brown brogues on," I said. "I was embarrassed by my muddy sneakers."

Gaurav returned and flipped his laptop open. "Okay, this is how the pros do it. Poppy, I need to know every little thing about Arnold Bentley that you can remember. No detail is too small."

I thought hard, but I really didn't know very much at all. I knew his wife's name, that he rented Broomewode Farm directly from Lord Frome, who was an ex-client of his. He drove an old Land Rover and had an amazing border collie named Sly. When he asked me for Arnold Bentley's approximate age, I guessed at early sixties. But it was hard to tell. To me, as soon as you started wearing cashmere and driving around in a Land Rover, you'd made it to grown-up status. In comparison, I still felt like a kid, rattling around in my battered Renault Clio, and most of my woolens came from Marks & Spencer and were definitely not cashmere.

Gaurav quietly tapped away, looking utterly absorbed in his screen, while I finished my wine. Hamish raised an eyebrow at me. "Proper little hacker we have here," he said, laughing before it turned into another sneeze. Florence jumped away from the table and came over to my side. "Safer over here," she whispered into my ear. I laughed, and we started to talk about tomorrow's final challenge, speculating about who might be going home.

"I don't want to be mean, because I think she's lovely, but Evie really does seem like the most obvious choice," Florence said.

I nodded. "I have to agree. She's clearly a great baker, but she loses it when the cameras are on. She has to learn to hold her nerve on this show."

Hamish made a sound a bit like a moan. "Don't forget my parsnip disaster. Why, oh, why, didn't I use something sensible? I was too clever for my own good. It's likely me as'll be sent home."

"We still have tomorrow," I reminded them. "Any of us could make the kind of mistake you can't recover from. Hamish, you'll feel better, and Evie could be brilliant. If she can get over her nerves on camera. Jonathon should stay away from her. I think he makes her worse. He's so much tougher on contestants than Elspeth." It was true. Although I'd busted him rehearsing his lines about fruit cakes, Jonathon did judge more harshly than Elspeth. Maybe I was biased, considering Elspeth was essentially my witch mom.

Gaurav looked up from his laptop and spun it round to

face the table. "I wonder if this had anything to do with his death."

The three of us stopped talking immediately and turned to stare at the screen. Gaurav had found an article in the London *Financial Times* from five years earlier about the downfall of an investment fund. "You'll see that Arnold Bentley was the owner of the firm. It went bankrupt, and his investors lost millions. He was investigated for fraud, but nothing was ever proven. It was put down to a bad economy and bad management." He hit a button and another article appeared. "And here's an article about a class-action suit. The investors got back ten pence on the pound."

"No!," said Florence, putting her hands to her chest. "He was an embezzler."

Gaurav shook his head. "Arnold Bentley lost his license, but fraud was never proven. The judge determined that he was too much of a risk taker with other people's money but not a criminal, so he avoided jail."

"Ten pence on the pound?" Hamish gave a low whistle. "Sounds criminal. What happened to the other ninety?"

"Let's not get carried away." I'd met him, and they hadn't. He'd seemed like a dull sort of man who'd done well in life and earned a quiet retirement. For some reason, when I thought of an embezzler, I pictured someone flashy and full of cheap charm. "That is certainly one big jump to a conclusion. I believe the judge and he was simply a bad investor, not a crooked one."

Hamish tried to say something but then blew his nose again. He sounded too sick to bake again tomorrow, but as we all knew, the show had to go on. In a thick tone, he asked if there were any names mentioned.

Gaurav nodded, looking quite pleased to be asked. "Most of his investors were small—people who had their retirement money and children's education funds invested—but among his principal investors were Lord and Lady Frome. The same Lord and Lady Frome who own Broomewode Hall."

"YES," I said. "They rented the farm to the Bentleys. For a modest price, according to Susan. Why would they do that if they were enemies?"

Florence said, in her rich, theatrical voice, "Perhaps Lord and Lady Frome offered them the farm to get them close, plotting ways for their death. I studied a play like that once. And, as we bakers know, revenge is a dish best served cold."

CHAPTER 10

"Oh, not you again," I said, opening the door to my room. Gerry was practicing levitating from my bed to the ceiling.

He looked delighted to see me. "Hello, stranger. It's like you don't even sleep here. I was going to float down to the dining room and haunt you all, but I couldn't be bothered."

Thank goodness for that. "It's been quite the day," I said, slipping off my boots and flopping onto the bed beside him.

"Well, I spent my evening hovering around the kitchen. I miss steak and kidney pie. And mashed potatoes. And buttery cabbage. Oh, and stay away from the bread pudding tomorrow." He put a finger to the side of his nose. "And that's all I'm saying."

"But Gerry," I said, sighing, "you can't taste anything. Why bother?"

"My taste buds might be blinkered, but my memory is perfectly intact. It's torture, knowing that all those delightful dishes are being prepared downstairs and I can't enjoy a single one."

"Well, believe me, there are worse things." I paused, wondering if telling Gerry there had been another death might cause more trouble. But since he'd soon find out anyway, I took a deep breath and relayed the day's events for the third time this evening. It definitely didn't get any easier.

"Holy smokes!" Gerry exclaimed. "I bet you any money it was that oaf of an electrician, Aaron Keel. I've been watching him, you know, and I'm telling you, that guy is suspect. I know Marcus Hoare sabotaged my ovens, but there's something I don't like about Aaron." He shook his head. "Nope. I don't trust him as far as I could throw him."

"That's not very far, Gerry," I reminded him. "And it's no good jumping to conclusions like that. Why would he kill Arnold Bentley? If it was even murder. Why Arnold was anywhere near those bees is still a mystery."

Gerry stroked his chin in mock detective style. "Another case for me to solve."

I didn't remind Gerry that it was actually Gina and I who'd apprehended his murderer. We'd sat on his back and restrained him with a celebrity baker's scarf, no less.

"Look," I said. "You need to stay out of trouble if you're to have any hope of passing on. The police are already investigating. Leave it to the professionals."

"Oh, you mean Mr. Dimples? Don't blush. I've seen the way you look at him."

Yeesh. Gerry was fast becoming the brother figure I never wanted. I needed to get him on another subject, so I told him that Florence's theory was that Lord and Lady Frome had given the Bentleys the farm for a good price to lure them here and then waited until enough time had passed that they could do away with Arnold Bentley. Him having an allergy to bees had played right into their hands.

Gerry looked interested. "I'd float up there and snoop if I could, but you know I'm tethered to the inn and the baking tent. If you can lure the Fromes into the pub, I could sit at their table and eavesdrop on their conversation."

"Would they really talk about the man they murdered in the local pub?" I'd never seen them leave their property. They seemed so snooty and full of themselves, I could not picture them in the local pub, never mind gossiping over their shepherd's pie and Guinness.

"Probably not. Do you have a better idea?"

"I am determined to get inside Broomewode Hall. If I could get inside, maybe I could gather some clues."

Gerry flipped upside down and hung from the light fixture by his shiny white sneakers. "That seems as likely as them coming to the pub for dinner."

"True. There must be some way we can at least work out their movements. Susan Bentley said the bees were fine at nine this morning. It wasn't until the afternoon that she noticed the hive was down and Arnold on the ground. So, where were the Fromes between those hours?"

"How are you going to find that out?"

"I don't know."

"Wait!" He tried to snap his fingers, but the result was soundless. "That fellow who's been hanging around in the pub, I heard him say he was going to visit the Champneys and try and sell them his ridiculous tires."

"Really?" Sometimes Gerry could actually be helpful.

"Yeah. He was dressed up all smart, and Eve behind the bar complimented him. He told her he was meeting with the

Fromes and to wish him luck. She not only did, but she gave him a stone."

"She gave him a stone? Like a rock?"

"No, like that." He pointed to my throat, where Elspeth's amethyst lay.

"A crystal, you mean?"

He flipped himself back so I could look at him without craning my neck. That was better. "Yes. Told him to keep it in his pocket and it would bring him luck."

"Did he say what time he was meeting them?"

I felt that Gerry was losing interest in the conversation, which made him a very poor sleuth. He was more interested in trying to make his spectral body into a perfect circle. "You'd better ask Eve."

"If I can find out, then we could determine part of their movements during the critical hours between happy, contented bees and living Arnold and angry, disturbed bees and dead Arnold."

"Okay, here's the plan. Go see them and drop heavy hints that you know what they did. Then get them down to the pub so I can eavesdrop. Once you've got them nervous that you know what they've done, they won't be able to talk about anything else."

It wasn't a bad idea, but how would I get the snooty Earl and Countess to a humble pub?

"They aren't the only suspects, you know." Maybe Gerry wasn't the world's greatest detective sidekick, but at least I could talk through my suspicions and get some feedback. When I could make him listen. "Gerry, take your feet out of your mouth and pay attention."

"Bet you can't do that," he said smugly.

"Put my foot in my mouth? I do it all the time." Like telling a detective I thought Arnold Bentley had been murdered. What had I been thinking? It not only wasn't my business, but it *was* his. I must have looked like an idiot, and Gerry was right, I did have a little crush on Detective Dimples, which I was definitely going to keep to myself.

"Okay," Gerry said, sitting properly on the edge of the bed. "Who else could have done it?"

"Peter Puddifoot."

"The Pudster. In the field. With the bees." He put his head to one side. "Doesn't quite have the right ring, does it?"

"Nevertheless, we both heard him and Arnold Bentley arguing. And he kicked Sly." To my mind, anyone who tried to hurt an animal was halfway to being a murderer. "Remember, I heard him shouting at Arnold that he should have had the farm when his father died. Well, assuming Susan Bentley decides not to stay on, the farm will once again be available. How convenient."

He nodded, actually giving me his full attention. "And he loves those bees."

I wouldn't go that far. I doubted Peter Puddifoot loved anything but himself and maybe Somerset cider. "He was certainly angry that they were being given away."

"To that pretty silver-haired bloke. I've seen him in the pub. He tries to fit in with the locals, but they make fun of him behind his back. Him with his five acres and the old smithy. He's been taking lessons, you know."

"Lessons? In beekeeping, you mean?"

"No. Blacksmithing. Likes to play with hot pokers. Make twee things. Garden ornaments, wind chimes and such."

Oh, dear. I could imagine how the locals might mock a

Londoner who'd come down to become a hobby blacksmith. Still, I thought it would be cool to have local artisans working the old ways. But then I was an outsider too.

Should I tell Gerry about Susan and Reg? I felt bad gossiping, but the best thing about Gerry as a confidante was that I was guaranteed he wouldn't pass on anything I told him. Which made him the perfect person to speculate with. "I saw Susan Bentley coming out of Reginald McMahan's cottage Friday afternoon. They looked pretty cozy."

Now my ghostly companion definitely looked interested. "What? You think they're having it on over the old forge? While the old man's tucked away with his Bovril and his EpiPens?"

I stared up at the ceiling, where a small crack meandered across one corner. "I have no idea. Certainly no proof, but he was the first person she called after she found her husband."

Gerry made a rude noise. The ghost's version of a snort. "No doubt she didn't need to use the phone. What do you bet, the old boy caught them at it and they decided to do away with him? Nothing easier. She could lure him down to the hives. Reg could be hiding behind one and push it over as soon as Arnold Bentley got near. Then all they had to do was grab his pen away from him and no more Arnold." He stretched out beside me once more. He was the most restless ghost.

"Did he have life insurance? Will she inherit a packet that she can enjoy with her lover?"

"No idea." But I bet the police would be looking at that angle.

"You said she seemed gutted to lose the Mayfair House and the Porsche."

"And don't forget the house in Saint-Tropez."

"Maybe she was angry that Arnold took away her lovely life and brought her down here, where she was driving a tractor instead of a shiny new sports car? Collecting eggs and scraping honey to make ends meet? She thought he owed her and decided to get the money back. Out of his hide."

"I guess it's possible. But Susan seemed so nice."

"Beware the nice ones. Remember when you all thought Gordon the soundman was so nice? And I got nicely barbecued."

Ouch. "Right. Good point." But how would we prove that Susan Bentley and Reginald McMahan had conspired to murder her husband? Oh, I sat up in bed so fast my head swam. "I saw him this afternoon. Reginald, I mean. He was watching the show being filmed."

"Hmm. Bunch of movie stars you are now. That's nice."

Okay, I felt bad that Gerry was permanently off the show, but he was messing with my concentration. "He was chatting to Eve. Then I saw him walk up toward Broomewode Manor."

"The manor or the farm?"

"That's the trouble. It's the same path. You turn left to get to the farm or continue straight to the Hall." I was thinking furiously. "And the timing would work. We still had the second challenge to film. He chatted to Eve, and then I saw him turn and walk up the path."

"Wonder what he and Eve were chatting about?"

"Me, too." I doubted it was about murder, but maybe he'd told Eve where he was going and why. It was possible. And I could casually bring him up in conversation and see if Eve knew anything.

"Of course, there were people coming and going all afternoon. Peter Puddifoot also went stomping up that path. I assumed he was going to complain about the spectators ruining his lawn. But maybe he didn't go to Broomewode Manor at all. Maybe he went to the farm."

"He definitely knew about Arnold Bentley's allergy to bees."

"The whole village must have known, the way those two were shouting about it."

"Seems like a lot of people had it in for the old codger," Gerry mused. "And with all the coming and going, the crew, and the spectators, it would have been easy to slip away and knock over a beehive." Now he sat up too. "Wait, what about the sound engineer? Crafty-looking little sod." He shook his head. "I never trust a man with a beard."

"Who? Robbie Denton?"

He shook his head. "And that's another thing I don't like. Robbie. What's wrong with Robert? Or Bob if you must?"

"I don't know, *Gerry.*"

"That's different. No one under a hundred is called Gerald. Seriously. I was named for my grandfather. But Robert's a fine name. What's he trying to prove by having a name like a little kid?"

"Gerry, I think you only have it in for poor Robbie because of his predecessor."

He shook his finger at me. "You mark my words. Keep an eye on little Robbie."

I was picturing the onlookers. Who else had been there? "Oh, that man who's trying to sell tires to the Fromes. He was there. He had a meeting with the earl. Maybe he saw something?"

"I doubt he saw the earl's money." Gerry shook his head.

"I could have told him not to waste his time there. The Fromes don't have that kind of money."

"No. Thanks to Arnold Bentley." And now we were back where we'd started with possible suspects in a possible murder.

~

I NEEDED to take a bath to wind down from the drama of the day so I told Gerry he'd have to vamoose. He pouted, but I threatened him with a blocking spell, which meant he'd never be able to talk with me again. Of course, I didn't know a spell like this or if one even existed, but I figured Elspeth must be doing something similar for Gerry not to realize who —or more like what—she was.

"But I'm bored," he complained. "Talking about murder is at least interesting."

"Go downstairs and eavesdrop in the pub. If word's got out about the death, and in a gossipy village like this one, it probably has, then everyone will be talking about it. Float around. Hear what you can and report back."

"I suppose I could."

"You are the best co-detective. You can see and hear things when no one realizes you're even there."

"Like the proverbial fly on the wall," he said gloomily. But he went.

~

WITH GERRY safely floating back downstairs to the pub, I shimmied out of my outfit, noticing that I had chocolate on the back of my silk shirt (how did I even manage to do that?) and switched on the radio. In my absence, it had been reset to a classical music station, and the lilting sound of a lone violin filled the room. It was beautiful and a little haunting, exactly suiting my mood.

I turned the brass taps of the bath and watched the water gush into the tub. Steam began to fill the room, and I found that the inn had also changed the miniature bottles of bubbles from rosemary and bay to prickly pear. I inhaled the sweet, fruity scent and was about to pour the lot into the bath when I noticed something strange about the water. It was swirling, rather than rising, like a gentle whirlpool.

I blinked. Was I so tired I was hallucinating now, or had that wine gone right to my head? I closed my eyes and opened them again. And that's when I saw the churning water suddenly still and an image appear on its surface.

At first it wasn't clear, just a shadowy outline, but then a familiar shape sharpened into focus. Although the room was steamy and hot, a chill spread through my body. It was the same heavily pregnant woman from my vision by the river at the footbridge near Broomewode Hall. My heart began to beat double time. Like before, the image was too shadowy for me to make out the woman's face, but I was hit with the sense that if I could, my own features would be present there. Was it my mother, or did I just want it to be? I still wasn't sure.

I leaned in closer, desperate for a glimpse of her face, but she remained hidden. And the water began to stir again, rippling and swelling, making the image seem frantic and wild. There was the sound of static, and then the radio went dead. I felt my eyes widen in fear. What was happening? And then I heard it, a soft voice calling to me. "Poppy, you're in danger, you're in danger. You must leave this place."

I was too startled to even try to reply, and by the time my mind woke up again to tell my mouth to try and speak to this apparition, as I had so many questions, the impression in the water had vanished. I reached out to touch where the woman's concealed face had been just seconds ago and yanked my hand back. The water had turned brutally cold.

I shivered as the radio sprang back to life and the sounds of a full orchestra crashed into the room. So much for a relaxing hot bath.

I pulled the plug and stared as the water swirled down the drain. If it had been my mother, her voice was gentle and lovely, full of tenderness and love despite the warning message. I felt exhilarated at hearing its sound for the first time, but this was tempered by a feeling of absolute dread. She had spoken to me only to warn me about impending danger. As if I wasn't aware that life could take a dramatic turn for the worse in a matter of seconds. I'd already come face-to-face with a murderer and seen my life flash before my eyes as I narrowly escaped being flattened by a crumbling tower.

I already knew that I had to be careful—Elspeth and Sgt. Lane were saying the same thing, so what else could my mom be trying to warn me about? Could more disasters be heading my way? Why else would she speak in my vision for the first time? I wished so hard that it had been to say something comforting or loving. Or even, "I like your hair like that, Pops." Anything but a warning.

And what if it wasn't my mother? I had a pretty good idea that being a witch meant I was more receptive to negative supernatural forces as well as the good ones. Was something toying with me? Frightening me for no reason? Pretending to be my mother?

I showered quickly and then slipped into pajamas, feeling fearful and unsettled.

Maybe if I concentrated on getting ready for tomorrow, I'd get out of this nervous funk I was in. Gateau wasn't around to comfort me. At that moment, I'd have welcomed Sly and his soggy ball for company. I even missed Gerry.

Resolutely, I opened the wardrobe and picked out the outfit Gina had helped me select for tomorrow's filming. I laid it neatly on the back of the chair. I loved the dark denim jeans and soft, ribbed pink sweater we'd settled on, but now all that preparation seemed silly. What did looking fashionable matter if I was in some kind of mortal danger? Elspeth's necklace was still around my neck, and I touched the purple stone and hoped that this, and keeping my wits about me, would be enough to help me through whatever might be coming my way.

Although I was exhausted, I had little hope for sleep now. I went to the window and opened it just enough that Gateau could slip back in whenever she was ready. I spent a moment looking out over the grounds. The moon was full, a huge silver orb suspended in the black sky, and it illuminated Broomewode Hall so that it seemed to shimmer.

I was so lost in my thoughts that I didn't know how long someone had been knocking on my door until I heard my name.

It was Elspeth. I raced over and flung open the door.

"Goodness," she said as I hugged her hard. "Whatever has happened? I would say that you look like you've seen a ghost if I didn't already know that was a common occurrence for you."

"I had a dreadful vision," I said, standing back and blushing a little. I sounded like a little kid running to mommy because she'd had a bad dream. It had become easy to forget that Elspeth wasn't just my witchy godmother, she was a celebrity, too, and we didn't know each other well enough for me to actually crush her in a bear hug. And on top of that, I was wearing red tartan pajamas and she was in a pair of perfectly pressed brown slacks and cream cashmere sweater. Over her arm, she carried a woolen coat. I felt like a total dork.

But instead of pulling back or looking offended, Elspeth shut the door and ushered me to the bed, while she settled in one of the armchairs. "Tell me what happened."

"It was my mother, I'm sure of it. No. I'm not sure. But it might be. But either way, she was warning me that I'm in danger. I don't know what's going on."

Elspeth frowned, and a flash of concern clouded her warm eyes. "Yes, I've had this strange feeling all evening, Poppy. Something isn't quite right. But I can't put my finger on what it is."

"You mean you haven't heard about Arnold Bentley?"

"Arnold who?"

Once more I explained about the death by bees I'd witnessed this afternoon.

"Oh, my poor Poppy. What a dreadful day. It nearly over-shadows your delightful Gooseberry Upside-Down Cake and that well-deserved win."

Yep. Almost.

She nodded, as though she'd come to a decision. "Put

some clothes on and come with me. It's a full moon, and I'm taking you to your first magic circle." She smiled conspiratorially as I just gawped at her. "Put on something warm, as we've a bit of a walk and it's a chilly evening."

I didn't even have the words to ask what happened at a magic circle. Instead, I grabbed a sweater and some fresh underwear from the wardrobe and stepped into the bathroom to pull on my old jeans and run a brush through my hair. I peered at the mirror. My eyes were red from tiredness, my skin paler than usual, too. But I was also excited. Would a magic circle finally give me an insight into what it really meant to be a witch? Would I meet some of the coven Elspeth had told me were drawn to Broomewode? And, most importantly, could I trust myself not to say or do something embarrassing? Hmm, the jury was out on that one.

I was glad now I'd brought so many clothes as I put on a warm sweater and over it, a navy woolen coat.

We left the inn in comfortable silence. Okay, Elspeth seemed comfortable, and I was definitely nervous. A man had died today under suspicious circumstances, and I'd been warned I was in danger.

Still, I gamely followed Elspeth as she guided me onto a narrow pebbled path, lit by old-fashioned caged lanterns. Whitebeam trees flanked either side of the path like they were guarding it, and their puffy leaves swayed gently in the breeze. We walked away from the inn and the manor house, on a path that grew rougher and headed into woods. The lanterns stopped, and we had only the pale silver moonlight to guide us. We climbed a short hill, and the path meandered through thick trees until we came out into a clearing, and in the middle was a circle of standing stones.

It looked like a small and long-forgotten version of Stonehenge. I'd been to the famous stone circle, of course, as a tourist, but since living here, I'd discovered there were stone circles all over the British Isles. Some in better repair than others.

This one had a decent-size head stone and a rough circle of stones, some fallen over, some so badly weathered by time and the elements that they were like half-melted snowmen. Gaps showed where stones had once been.

"The local people used to take the stone and break it up to build houses and fences and things," Elspeth told me in a low voice. She shook her head. "They had no respect for the traditions and the old ways. It's much better now. These circles are protected by law." She sighed. "Still, the damage is done."

"I can't believe I didn't even know this was here. No one's mentioned it, either."

"Sometimes we only notice the things we're already looking for," she said cryptically, with a small smile playing around her lips. "Brace yourself, Poppy, you're about to meet some of the Broomewode Coven. You must take an oath of secrecy, but try to keep your countenance, dear. You may be surprised by what you see."

I TOOK a deep breath as Elspeth led me into the center of the circle, where a group of women had gathered.

"Good evening. I think some of you already know Poppy Wilkinson."

I felt my mouth drop open as Eve grinned back at me. To

her right was the old woman who had called me Valerie in the pub last week, and her daughter, who raised her hand in hello. And I recognized one of the cooks from Broomewode Hall who'd been chopping up vegetables when I'd visited Katie Donegal. I shook my head in disbelief.

In total, there were eight women and one man, some of whom I'd never seen before. Were they all witches? Or was a magic circle just people interested in magic and spells and not those who'd been born witches? Why, oh why hadn't I asked Elspeth more questions before we got here?

Each of the witches came forward and took my hands, whispering welcome and each of them saying, "Blessed Be." I had always felt so different, growing up an only child, the girl who started life in an apple box, and with the unfortunate trick of seeing the dearly departed—after they'd departed. But now, within this strange circle of stones, overlooked by the heavy moon, as these women and man came forward, offering me welcome, I felt for the first time as though I belonged.

Someone emerged from another path, and when she grew closer, I recognized Susan Bentley. She stared straight ahead, not seeming to focus on anything in particular. It was a lot like how she'd looked down at her tea earlier, as if in a trance. Was Susan part of the coven, too? It was fair to say that my mind was blown.

I was no longer the center of attention. The women who'd already greeted me now went to offer support to the new widow, while the few who still wanted to greet me did so and then moved on to comfort Susan Bentley. Now I knew what she'd meant when she said she had sisters in the area. Of course. I stood back, partly because I was brand new but also because I wasn't convinced Susan Bentley was as much a grieving widow as she pretended. Where did Reg the artisan blacksmith fit into all of this? A guy who forged iron as a hobby must be pretty strong. Certainly strong enough to knock over a beehive and drag an unwilling allergy sufferer to his death.

I was even more shocked when Jonathon strode into the circle. I felt the rustle of emotion and suspected he hadn't been expected or wasn't as familiar to them as Elspeth.

Eve fetched two cloth shopping bags she'd left beside the head stone and from them drew large candles. She began to place them in a circle within the stones. When she was done, she looked to Elspeth, who invited us all to enter the circle. Then, with a graceful gesture, she made a circling motion with her outstretched finger, and each of the candles sprang to light.

Even though there was a slight breeze blowing, the wicks burned with a steady flame.

I really wanted to sit down, put my head between my knees and wait for reality to return.

"Sisters and brothers, we are gathered here tonight to create good energy and form a sacred space to provide our dear sister Susan Bentley magical protection and aid her dear departed husband, Arnold Bentley, in his journey to the other side."

Elspeth reached out and took my hand and that of the woman next to her. Everyone followed suit, and we made a ring. A gentle ripple of electricity fizzed in my hand and sent waves up into one arm and then out of the other. I had a sudden rush of compassion for Susan, as if her pain was now mine and it was me who was in mourning. The witches closed their eyes, and I felt my own lashes fluttering on my cheeks, too.

Elspeth began to speak again, but this time it was in a language I didn't understand. It sounded ancient and yet familiar, as if I'd heard it somewhere before but the memory had escaped me. The women joined Elspeth now, echoing her words in a slow chant that rippled through the circle like a murmur. I opened my eyes, and that's when I saw him.

In the middle of the circle, hovering in what had been an empty space just moments before, was the flickering outline of a man. He was tall and slender, wearing a brown robe, possibly a cassock, like monks wear, and he was smiling at me like I was an old friend. It was like a hologram, beamed in from another place. Was I hallucinating? I couldn't stop staring. The man nodded again before disappearing.

I swallowed hard and looked about the circle. The women all had their eyes closed, and Susan was weeping silently. I had absolutely no idea what I had just seen. But I did know one thing for sure: That man had known me—was he here for Susan Bentley, or was he here for me?

CHAPTER 11

*W*hen my alarm screeched at seven-thirty a.m., I groaned. How could it be morning already? I'd barely got to bed at dawn. I rolled over, and there was a disgruntled meow. Gateau scrambled from my feet and rearranged herself at the bottom of the bed. She must have slipped back in during the night. Today was the final challenge in this week's baking contest. A pretty important day. But I couldn't focus on cakes. I was trying to process what had happened last night.

Elspeth had whisked me away again after the ceremony. When I asked who everyone was and if they were all witches, too, she told me that we'd have a proper chat after filming today. I had no choice but to be patient. In hindsight, what I really should have asked for was a deep sleep potion. I'd woken up in fits and starts for the few hours I had to sleep, the events of the weekend playing out in surrealistic dreams, with odd fragments of bodies and wild splashes of color.

I dragged my weary body to the bathroom, still groggy and perplexed. I jumped in the shower and tried to mentally prepare myself to get out of the magic world and back into baking.

I dressed quickly and made my way downstairs to breakfast.

The dining room was already buzzing. I went straight to the buffet table and heaped my plate with sourdough toast, little pats of butter and mini raspberry jams, and a bowl of Greek yogurt with fresh berries. A steaming cup of strong black coffee, and I was starting to feel like a human again.

Sadly, the same could not be said for Hamish. He coughed his way through breakfast. I had no idea how he could breathe properly, let alone conjure up a show-stopping cake. But that gave me an idea: What if I could help Hamish out with a spell of some kind to nuke that nasty cold? I'd speak to Elspeth before filming began.

I sat next to Florence and Maggie, avoiding the spare chairs around Hamish, and the four of us chattered about our recipes. I liked how we'd made a little group, and I had a hard time remembering that my new friends were actually my competition. I'd have to find some fighting spirit inside me when we got inside the tent.

I was about to head to my room to brush my teeth when Elspeth walked in. She greeted the bakers with a smile and inquired how everyone had slept. She looked radiant, like she'd had twelve hours' sleep.

When no one was looking, Elspeth pressed something into my hand under the table. "Here," she said, her voice a conspiratorial whisper. "I made this for Hamish last night, the poor lamb. It's a special tonic. A few reviving herbs and a little pinch of something else." She glanced around as though worried a camera might be on her. "I can't be seen helping any contestants, but if you give him one of these to dose himself, Hamish's symptoms should disappear within the hour. Tell him it's a recipe your great aunt used to give you when you were a child. Just add it to a glass of water." Before I could reply, she'd walked away.

I opened my hand to see two small glass vials filled with a greenish liquid. I held it up to the light, wondering what magic it contained, when Hamish looked over curiously, I said. "Ah, this is for you," I said, handing him one of the vials. "It's my great aunt's cure-all cold medicine. Just mix it with water. It always worked wonders for me. I thought you'd need it for today."

"Oh, Poppy, how kind," he said, blowing his nose for the fifth time that morning. "What's in it?"

"Just a blend of special herbs and my magic touch," I added, not able to help myself.

He poured himself a glass of water and tipped the contents of the vial into its midst. The green liquid swirled and turned a beautiful emerald color. He drank the lot down. "Here's hoping."

Hamish glanced behind me. "I hope I haven't passed this thing on to a helpless stranger."

I craned my neck in the direction he indicated, and was surprised to see Bob Fielding, the tire salesman, looking pretty dejected. He had a scarf wrapped around his neck and was bundled up in a navy cable knit jumper, and he was shivering. I was astonished. How could anyone be that cold when I was sitting here in a thin top and was perfectly warm? I decided to go and speak with him and offer my second vial of tonic.

"Um, excuse me," I said, feeling rather British. "But I

couldn't help but notice you've got a bad cold. My friend Hamish—we're on the baking show—well, he has a terrible cold too, and I made him this." I stuck out the vial of green liquid. "It's an old family tonic for colds. It really helps."

The man looked surprised but gave me a crooked smile. He didn't look as sick as Hamish, but there was still something peaky about his face. "How kind, thank you." He didn't reach for it, so maybe he thought drinking green liquid out of an unlabeled bottle provided by a complete stranger was a bad idea. I gave him what I hoped was a trustworthy smile. "I'm Poppy Wilkinson."

"I'm Bob Fielding. I sell top-of-the-line tires. Was that your Land Rover out in the parking lot?"

I put the vial on the table and chuckled. "No. Mine's the sad, tiny blue car. And I bought tires for it last year." When they were deeply discounted.

"Well, when you win the challenge, get famous and upgrade your car to something splashy, give me a call." He passed me a business card.

Here was the opening I'd been looking for. Up close, he looked to be in his late forties, maybe early fifties. His brown hair had threads of gray at the temples, and his skin was mottled red from his cold. "I'm guessing it wasn't me you came to see."

He shook his head. "I met with Lord Frome, in fact. He's bought a lovely set of tires for his car and a set for his wife. I'm just waiting until Monday for the check."

Did the Earl of Frome really not have internet banking? Or was he so tight for money that he had to go to the bank to figure out how to buy the tires. Eve had said he was too poor to buy tires, but she'd also suggested that he and the missus spent more than they earned. Buying overpriced tires seemed in keeping.

"Good luck."

"Thank you. And thanks for this." Then, while I watched, he poured a glass of water, tipped the liquid into it and drank the potion down. "Not bad," he said when he was done. "Tastes a bit like mint."

Florence called me from across the room, and I excused myself. "You'll be feeling better in no time."

I caught up to Florence, and she linked my arm. "He's a little old for you, Pops, don't you think?"

I shook my head. "You know it's perfectly normal to talk to the opposite sex without flirting. Perhaps you should try it."

"Never!" She laughed, shaking out her mane of red curls, and we made our way to hair and makeup, the final step before the showstopper challenge.

JILLY AND ARTY exchanged a sly glance before Jonathon and Elspeth swept into the tent. Had anyone else noticed this budding romance, or was it just me? When I took a look around, all of the bakers' faces were trained on the clock on the wall, stern and troubled, waiting for the moment we could begin the final challenge. This one was make or break, and afterward, someone would be sent home.

Hamish looked worried. I suspected he'd never look at another parsnip as long as he lived. Evie tied up her apron with determination. She knew she was in trouble and was going to give it her all. Truth was, any one of us could have a disaster today and be saying goodbye to the other contestants, our workstation and the judges. I just wanted to get on with it. My fingertips were tapping impatiently on the smooth white workstation surface. We were made up, mic'd up, and ready to go.

Hamish saw me watching him and quickly came over to my station. "I already feel better. What was in that stuff? It's magic." And it was true. His nose had stopped streaming, and the color had returned to his face. Elspeth was truly magic. I'd have to see if she'd show me how to mix up a little tonic of my own.

The cameras followed Elspeth, her pale complexion powdered to perfection under the warm tent lights.

"Bakers," Elspeth said, addressing the room with a warm smile, "it's that time again. For today's showstopper, you must bake a cake themed around festivals and rituals. This could be anything from Easter, with its traditional chocolate Easter eggs, to October's harvest festival, full of wonderful produce from the earth. How you approach this challenge is entirely up to you, but we urge you to remember the basics as well as wow us with your creativity. Don't sacrifice taste for flair. We want rich buttercreams, lovely textures, and a good marriage of flavors." She paused and looked at each of us in turn. "Bakers, as ever, I wish you all the luck in the world, and I look forward to tasting each of your offerings."

Arty stepped forward. "All right, bakers. Your time starts... On your marks, get set, bake!"

And here it was: the cold dread, the rush of nerves, the sudden emptying of my mind. Actually, that wasn't true—my mind was too busy with other things to focus on my recipe. I was haunted by the scene of Susan bent over her husband's body; the terrible watery warning from the woman in my bath time vision; the smiling man in the magic circle, flickering like a hologram. I took a deep breath. All this could wait. It was showstopper time.

I'd spent ages deliberating about this one with Gina. I remembered our childhood trips to the neighboring village of Lacock to celebrate Beltane, the Gaelic May Day festival. Lacock was beautiful. Graceful medieval houses lined the narrow lanes and cobbled streets, and it was nestled in acres of unspoiled countryside. Lacock Abbey was a famous landmark often seen in films and TV shows. The entire town was now looked after by the British National Trust to make sure that its historic charm remained intact. Gina and I had loved going there for the May Day festival—it was like traveling back in time, and her dad had told us the history of the festival, which was dying out in England.

May Day used to be a very special day on the calendar, especially for those in the countryside, because it marked the beginning of summer and when cattle were driven out to pastures. Rituals were performed to protect the cattle, crops and people and to encourage growth. When night fell, special bonfires were lit, and their flames, smoke and ashes were deemed to have protective powers. People would leap over the flames.

We loved the mystery of these tales. Any fires lit in the houses would be put out and then lit again from the Beltane bonfire. The celebration would finish with a feast, and doors, windows, and livestock would be decorated with yellow May flowers.

Gina's dad would relay all this information in his kind but booming voice, and I imagined it in intricate detail.

Nowadays, the idea of a May Day festival had died out, but Lacock and other small villages still paid homage to summer and had a fete of sorts, with food and dancing around a maypole.

So my showstopper today was going to be a tribute to those happy childhood days. They seemed so long ago now, but that feeling of warmth and security was palpable as I finally got my act together and began to make my lemon and almond sponge. The plan was to make a marzipan maypole as a centerpiece and little yellow May flowers to decorate the base.

Around me, all kinds of interesting cakes were beginning to take form. Maggie was making some beautiful hand-painted Easter eggs. Gaurav and Evie were both doing their interpretation of a fruity Christmas cake, and I could see lengths of gorgeous red and green velvet ribbon on Evie's table. She was upping her game, that was for sure.

Florence was making an apple and cinnamon cake with cream cheese frosting for harvest festival. I could smell the mix of spices she was folding into her batter, and honestly, I was salivating. If only I could be as good at baking as I was at eating, then I'd be sure to take the wining title today.

But my mind kept wandering. I couldn't focus. May was a traditional time of fertility, and the woman in my vision last night kept returning to me. What was she trying to warn me about? The last time I'd seen her, she'd been pregnant, and it seemed like she was running away from Broomewode Hall. But like Elspeth said, maybe we only notice what we are already looking for. Was the idea that this woman was my mother just a fantasy I'd conjured? Did I just *want* it to be true, rather than looking at the facts?

I was jolted out of my thoughts by Jonathon, who had, by the bemused expression on his face, just asked me a question. I blushed. "I'm so sorry. I was miles away."

"Hopefully miles away in some baking paradise?"

I cringed. Was that a joke? Maybe Jonathon should rehearse a few of those, too. I decided to save him from himself and launched into my explanation of the traditional Beltane May Day festival in England. I spun some well-rehearsed (that's how you do it, Jonathon) lines about local produce and celebrating the changing seasons, and Jonathon nodded encouragingly.

"That certainly is a unique take on the challenge, Poppy," Arty said, crashing into our conversation. "I don't think I've ever heard of a Beltane bonfire before. Great local knowledge for someone so young."

I swallowed hard. Patronizing much?

"May Day was an important part of my childhood, actually. I grew up nearby, before leaving for the States with my family, and I have many happy memories of taking trips to Lacock to watch the maypole dance."

"A pole dance? Doesn't sound very child-friendly," Arty snickered and wandered off, evidently pleased with himself. Jonathon and I shared an eye roll, and then he, too, left so that I could finish this monster cake I'd embarked on. Maybe three separate sponge layers was a little over the top, but I'd started now, and I had to see it through. I couldn't let myself down now, not after yesterday's mega win.

The marzipan took forever to roll out, but once the sponges were baked and cooled, I sandwiched them together with a layer of pale lemon buttercream and draped the marzipan over the top. Then I had to arrange the tiny figurines and erect the maypole in the center. I'd carefully cut thin strips of multicolored ribbon for the pole and began to weave them into the pole's ring. They weren't edible, of course, but they sure looked cute. At least a hundred times better than my icing Eiffel Towers. The next challenge was making the May flowers and painting them yellow with food dye.

Before I knew it, Jilly was clanging the gong and time was up. Phew. I'd really worked in a daze for the last hour and was surprised to see a finished cake in front of me. But boy, was I pleased! It might have been ambitious, but it paid off. The maypole was a little wonky, but I thought the overall effect was charming. Now it just had to taste good. I said a small prayer to the sponge gods that my crumb would be perfect and the buttercream light but decadent.

As each contestant lined up their cakes, I couldn't see a single one that didn't impress me. The competition was heating up. Evie, who we all knew was seriously struggling, had baked a stunning Christmas cake, decorated with sumptuous faux velvet fondant and a little manger.

Gaurav had gone the whole hog with his Christmas cake, with an entire nativity scene on the top. Florence's cake looked incredible. But it was Euan who really surprised me— for two reasons. Firstly, I'd totally forgotten that Euan was a beekeeper back in his native Wales. How this had eluded me with all the bad bee business going on this weekend, I didn't know. His showstopper explored the ritual of The Order of the Bees, which happens at summer solstice. On top of his honey-colored cake was a beehive, honeycomb, flowers, and tiny, perfectly striped bees. It was a masterpiece.

So when Elspeth crowned Euan the winner, no one was

surprised—except for Euan. He was wearing a red lumber-jack-style shirt, and his cheeks turned a shade to match. He even asked if they'd made a mistake.

"It's a wonderful cake, Euan," Elspeth said. "You should be very proud."

Florence turned to me and whispered, "It's the quiet ones you've got to watch out for. He came out of nowhere. We can't afford to get complacent."

"I don't know why you're worried," I said. "You came in second. Jonathon loved your cake. And I'm happy being third."

Florence lowered her voice to even more of a whisper, "You're right. It's Maggie who should be worried. She's slipping down. And poor old Hamish hasn't won a single round yet."

After the congratulations died down, the tent fell silent again as we waited for Elspeth to announce who was going home this week. Even though I'd baked my little heart out this weekend, I was still worried. Going home was so not an option for me. I had more to lose than anyone else here if I couldn't continue my time at Broomewode Hall.

But Jilly didn't draw out our misery. "The person we're going to be sending home today is a warm and wonderful human being, full of patience and heart. Unfortunately, the baking just wasn't where it needed to be for this show, so this week we'll be saying goodbye to Evie."

I breathed a sigh of relief. But poor Evie. You could tell she really was an excellent baker, just not good under pressure. We crowded round her, showering her with hugs and praise.

She wiped away a few tears with a tissue. "I'd just like to

say I've learned so much. It's felt like such a privilege to be in the tent. I really didn't think I would cope very well with the cameras, so it's kind of a miracle I made it this far! I'm proud of myself and want to thank everyone involved with the show for such an amazing experience."

The cameras stopped rolling, and we returned to our workstations to tidy the mess we'd made. I was bone-tired. But Euan's win had piqued my curiosity about what had happened to Arnold Bentley. I needed to know more about his beekeeping. I finished my cleaning double quick and went to congratulate him.

I told him how original his idea was and that I was fascinated by beekeeping. "Are you not afraid of getting stung?" I asked him. "Surely it must happen a lot if you're working with them every day?"

"Oh no, that almost never happens, and I've been keeping bees for decades. Bees are extremely docile creatures and only sting if they feel attacked."

I didn't know how to reply. Without knowing it, Euan had confirmed my worst fears. Arnold Bentley was far too afraid of bees to do anything close to attacking them—someone else must have been involved in his death.

CHAPTER 12

I left the tent and stood for a moment in the fresh air, taking deep lungfuls and trying to gather my thoughts. The sun was moving across the horizon, but it was still light, and the grounds of Broomewode Hall looked orange and glowing. I wondered how DI Hembly and Sgt. Lane were getting on in their investigation.

But there wasn't much I could do to help the investigation now. Instead, I figured it was high time I continued with my detective work into my own past.

I still had gooseberries for Katie Donegal. I'd take them up and see how her arm was healing. I knew she'd want all the details of Arnold Bentley's death, and maybe while we were gossiping, she'd offer up a little more information about the mysterious Valerie, the kitchen helper who'd disappeared twenty-five years ago and never been seen since. The woman I thought might be my birth mother.

I told Florence and the others I needed to stretch my legs for a bit and that I'd meet them back at the inn for an early supper before we all set off for our homes again.

By now, the short walk over to the manor house felt as familiar to me as the journey from my cottage to the grocery store. I loved the spring flowers that spilled out of the garden beds as I approached Broomewode Hall. I was no longer afraid of the giant building. If anything, my determination to get inside and demand some answers was growing stronger all the time.

To the left of the house, I saw a familiar figure in the garden. It was Benedict, dressed again in gardener's clothes and fixing a fence that separated two parts of the garden from one another. I had no idea why it was that the Champneys could afford to employ a butler, yet their only son and heir ended up responsible for yard maintenance.

"Hello there," I called out.

He raised his bent back and turned to look at me, shielding his eyes from the sun.

"Aha, you again," he said, smiling, his brown eyes crinkling at the corners. "You aren't half attached to this place."

I gestured to his fence. "So are you."

"I don't live here all the time. In case you were wondering."

"No judgment from me. I'm actually here to see how Katie is recovering and to bring her some of the gooseberries I picked. I do hope she's feeling better?"

"Well, I think so. But Katie isn't here."

My heart sank into my boots. Why, oh why was it so difficult pinning Katie down? She had a broken arm and should have been here resting in her quarters. It was like she knew when I was coming and hotfooted it out of Broomewode Hall.

I must have looked dismayed because he said, "Mother gave her a holiday. She couldn't manage with only one arm, and she kept getting in the way of the temporary cook who was covering her shifts, bossing her about in the kitchen. Too many cooks and all that..." He trailed off and shrugged.

So Lady Frome had given Katie a holiday. Of course, it made sense since the woman couldn't do her duties, but it couldn't have come at a worse time for me.

"Katie booked herself a flight to Ireland. She's visiting her family and will recuperate over there."

"Oh," I said, dismayed. "How long will she be there for?"

"She's not expected back for several weeks."

I was stunned. There went my brilliant plan of pumping Katie for information about Valerie. Now what?

"Here are the gooseberries that I nearly got killed picking." I knew I must have sounded a bit sulky, but I couldn't contain my disappointment.

"About that," Benedict continued, "we've got the building surveyor coming tomorrow to look at that tower. If it's not safe, it may have to come down."

"Oh, no," I cried before I could stop myself. "It's so beautiful. Surely it can be saved?"

He made a face. "Romantic old wrecks cost a lot of money in upkeep." He leaned on his spade and gazed out toward the old tower. "It was only checked a few months back. I can't work out how a large chunk of stone could have fallen like that, right when you were picking fruit at its base."

When his eyes turned back to me, I felt that he was accusing me somehow. Like I'd knocked into the tower and made the stone topple.

As he had done, I looked at the lonely tower. I wondered if he was telling the truth. Had the tower been sound only a few months ago? And if so, what did that mean? Could there have been intent behind that accident? Perhaps Arnold Bentley's killer had believed it was him at the base of that tower. I heard again the whispered voice warning me of danger. Could that tumbling stone have been intended for me? It didn't make any sense, any more than killing poor Arnold Bentley made sense.

My mind began to whir. What if Arnold's killer had been tracking the couple? Susan was at the farm when I went to the tower, collecting eggs. So then if the killer went to the tower, they might reasonably believe the figure at its base must be her husband. I'd been bent down picking fruit. And Sly was with me. It would have looked pretty compelling to someone from afar.

But if all this was true—and it was still a stretch—who would want Arnold and Susan Bentley dead?

Even more puzzling, who would want me dead?

Benedict put his gardening gloves back on. The sun was beginning to set, and everything was cast in an orangey haze. The temperature was dropping, too, and I shivered in my top. I'd all but bashed into Benedict coming away from the farm on the day of the falling stone. Could he have toppled the stone? Who knew the place and its weaknesses better than he did? Was there something about me that threatened Benedict Champney? I was probably being hysterical, but that vision haunted me coming on top of my near-death experience. I really needed to find out more about that woman and the past. I touched the amethyst, hoping very much that the protective spell was full strength.

"Will Susan have to move now her husband's dead?"

His brows rose at my question. I suppose it was nosy. "It's just that I know your father was an acquaintance of Mr.

Bentley before they moved here, and that's how they ended up at the farm."

"Yes, that's right. But we're hardly going to throw Mrs. Bentley off the farm just because her husband's gone. She can stay as long as she likes. Though I suspect she might not want to continue living in the place where her husband passed."

"That's very kind of you. Especially as I also heard that your family lost a lot of money when Arnold Bentley's firm went belly-up."

Benedict stiffened. I think I might have gone a bit too far with that last comment.

"You sound like the police," he said, his voice now rigid with enforced politeness. I thought he'd ignore me and go back to his gardening until I went away, but instead he turned back. "I've heard the rumors. But Bentley made sure my parents got out in time. They didn't make any money with him, but they didn't lose any either. Poor old Arnold had it much worse than us. And that's why my parents gave him the farm for very low rent. My father, in particular, had a real fondness for the chap."

I handed over the gooseberries, though I had no idea who was going to make jam with Katie gone, and told him that I was going to head back to the inn to have an early dinner with the other bakers before we all left for the weekend. He didn't look heartbroken to see me leave.

As I walked back, I couldn't stop wondering if Benedict was telling the truth. He certainly wasn't a straightforward character. Charming and a little handsome, I supposed, but I didn't doubt that he felt the need to protect his family's reputation. I wondered if he'd told me the truth about the family finances. Perhaps he hoped I'd spread this new rumor and it would cancel out the other.

But if I was to believe Benedict, then the Champneys certainly had no motive to murder Arnold. So who did?

I stopped walking. Straight ahead was the inn—friends, a warm dining room, and a tasty meal. But if I turned right, then the path would take me to Broomewode Farm. And maybe some answers.

Right it was.

CHAPTER 13

took out my phone and texted Gaurav to see if he could use his super tech search skills to find a list of the people who lost their money when Arnold Bentley's firm collapsed.

A minute later my phone rang.

"Poppy, where are you?" Gaurav asked, sounding concerned. "There'll be thousands of people affected by the collapse of Bentley's firm."

Oh. I hadn't thought of that. I nibbled at my lip and thought. "Can we narrow it down geographically?" I asked. "Start with locals and work out from there."

There was silence on the end of the line.

"What about lawsuits? I'm sure Susan said there'd been court battles. Can you get me information on that?"

"Shouldn't you be practicing for next week's baking challenge and leaving the police work to the police?"

He was right, but I felt compelled to understand what had happened. I'd been there when the man died. I wanted to help his widow get some answers as to why.

When I reached Broomewode Farm, I couldn't help giving a scared glance toward the tower that had nearly killed me. It looked lonely and lovely in the fading light. The fallen stone remained among the gooseberries, though, a grim reminder of my close call.

I heard Sly before I saw him. A loud, happy woof, and then there he was, bounding toward me in the half light, a joyous bundle of black and white fur. I couldn't stay morose when he was bounding around me, letting me know he was So Happy To See Me!

"Hi, boy," I said, bending down to stroke his nose. "It's good to see my canine guardian angel again, that's for sure."

He barked and nudged my ankles, herding me toward the house. It felt eerie being back here again, and I was worried that maybe the shady circumstances surrounding Arnold's death meant he hadn't passed over. Like my dear undeparted Gerry. I didn't think I could handle another haunting on the grounds of Broomewode Hall. I kept on the alert, expecting to see Arnold's ghost around every corner, but after a lap around the farmhouse, the coast was clear. Phew. I couldn't imagine anything worse than communing with someone who'd died at the hands of their worst fear. Just the thought gave me the heebie-jeebies.

There was police tape all around the beehives, but the fallen hive had been put upright again, I was pleased to see. Bee-wise, the farm was back to normal.

The farmhouse was dark except for one square window, which I recognized as the kitchen. I went to the side door and knocked. "Susan? It's Poppy."

"It's open," a frail voice said.

I took a deep breath and braced myself. I didn't have much experience dealing with the recently bereaved. It was the other side of things that I was good at.

I found Susan sitting at the kitchen table, dressed in jeans and an oversize cream sweater. Her short hair was sticking up in tufts. She didn't look up as I came in, preoccupied by stacking some jars on the table.

"I thought I'd come to check in with you," I said softly. "See how you're getting on. It was a surprise to see you last night. Sorry we didn't get a chance to talk."

Susan finally looked up at me. Her skin was pale and creased with worry. Her eyes were bloodshot, with bluish circles beneath them, and the tip of her nose was red. She looked like she'd been crying all day. "That's very kind. I could do with some company."

When I saw what was on the table, I was taken aback. Susan was arranging jars of honey into stacks and placing them into wooden crates. My expression must have given away how weirded out I felt, seeing her handling goods made by the very bees that killed her husband.

She gestured at the table and shrugged. "I think I'm still in shock. I don't know what to do with myself. I keep walking around this massive house aimlessly. What am I supposed to do without Arnold? It all feels so meaningless. So I decided to go ahead with the farmer's market, which had been arranged for next weekend. That's what all the honey is for—we have a stall booked. We usually sell out." She trailed off.

Sly went over to Susan and sat by her side, his big brown eyes watching her closely. When she reached out automatically to pat his head, his tail thumped the flagstone floor.

I told her that she didn't need to explain anything to me. Whatever helped her cope was surely a good thing.

"Susan, about last night. I couldn't believe how many women were in that circle. Are you...are you like me?" She gave me her full attention then and smiled. "Yes, Poppy. You didn't know?"

"Honestly, I'm not sure I know my madeleines from my macaroons right now." I looked at the dog, who'd herded me out of danger. I suspected he was more than a herder of sheep and chaser of slobbery balls. "Does that make Sly your familiar?"

"He is and he isn't," Susan replied. "As you'll have noticed, he senses a sympathetic spirit and connects with people. I believe if I moved or something happened to me, he'd quickly settle into a new home. But yes. He's my familiar. And I think that haughty and rather angry kitten is yours?"

Gateau was nothing but sweet with me, but she'd definitely shown a tough side with Sly. I nodded. "I didn't realize it at first. This is all very new to me."

"Let me make you some coffee. It will give me something to do. And then we can talk."

Susan's motions were slow and considered. She looked at the kettle for an age, as if she'd never seen one before, and then remembered it needed filling. We were both silent as the water bubbled and boiled.

I turned my attention to Sly and stroked his soft neck. "Don't tell Gateau," I whispered, "but I do think you are a very handsome, helpful familiar. Susan is lucky to have you." He gave my hand a long lick and then ambled over to Susan.

My phone buzzed, and I apologized to Susan. It was

Gaurav. She told me to take the call. I wandered into the hallway and picked up the phone excitedly.

"Have you found anything?" I asked.

"I think so, but there's a couple of things that just don't make sense. I'm going to screenshot what I found online and send it to you now. See what you make of it? But Poppy, please be careful. We don't really know what we're getting into here. Don't take any chances."

I thanked him and promised I'd be careful and then hurried back to the kitchen. When my phone dinged again a moment or two later, I opened the text and was taken aback by what I saw. But there was no time to contemplate Gaurav's findings, as Susan handed me a heavy ceramic mug filled with steaming black coffee.

Susan offered me the milk jug, but I shook my head. She poured a glug into her mug, seemingly mesmerized by the way the milk swirled into her coffee. After a few seconds, she gathered herself and asked me how I was.

I told her that I was confused, troubled by what happened to Arnold. It still didn't make sense to me that her very allergic husband had been anywhere near the bees. "And why wasn't he carrying an EpiPen? I've been trying to figure out if Arnold might have had any enemies. Maybe the accident with the tower wasn't an accident at all." I hesitated to add any more stress onto the grieving widow, but I felt she needed to know the truth about her husband's death.

"Yes, the police have the same queries about that," Susan said, stirring her coffee dejectedly, the spoon clanging against the sides.

"Do you think someone might have had a vendetta

against Arnold—something to do with the business failing, maybe? I know there was a lot of money involved."

Susan took a long sip of her coffee and sighed. "I never knew much about Arnold's business or that it was in trouble. He was very private about work, and to be honest, I didn't take much of an interest. I had the houses to run and friends, and of course, even in London I grew herbs and supervised the garden. I was always busy."

"It must have been a shock to lose everything and come here." Once more, I had to wonder if she was so angry with her husband that she'd helped his end along. Not every witch was a good witch.

"We never would have moved to the farm if we hadn't been desperate, and while Arnold hated it, I thrived. I have sisters here, and the herbs are powerful. I'm a reasonably good herbalist. And you? What are your gifts, little sister?"

I looked at her, startled. No one had ever addressed me as little sister before, not even Gina, even though we'd been attached at the hip as kids. I let my suspicions go for a moment and enjoyed the feeling of being connected. Like I'd come home.

I blurted out, "I sometimes communicate with the departed."

Susan's head snapped up. "You do? Have you—"

I hastened to assure her that I hadn't seen or heard a peep from her husband. She seemed happy. "He's passed over, then."

"Yes, he's not restless. I also think that perhaps I have some talent for uncovering the truth around suspicious deaths."

She looked surprised, as well she might. I'd had no idea those words were about to come out of my mouth. How many murders had I solved? One. With a lot of help. But Arnold's death bothered me on many levels, especially as I, too, had nearly met my end here on the farm.

"Well, I hope you'll find out who did this to Arnold," Susan said, tears forming in her eyes. "It won't bring him back, but it will give me some satisfaction, I suppose. Not knowing is the worst."

There was a knock on the kitchen door, and the nice lady from the gift shop was there, holding muffins still steaming with warmth. "Oh," she said when she saw me. "I hope I'm not intruding?"

"Not at all. Poppy, this is Eileen Poole, she runs the gift shop."

"Yes, we've met."

The old woman smiled at me. "And did the quince jelly help?"

"I hope so."

She went over to Susan and took her hand. "You'll get through this, my dear. You've got the whole village as your family, now."

I could tell that Eileen Poole was in no hurry to leave, so I said my goodbyes.

I could tell that Sly was torn. He wanted to come with me, and he needed to stay with Susan. "Good boy," I whispered, giving him a final pat. He was so good. He didn't even have his ball with him, perhaps feeling that running and playing were inappropriate in this time of grief.

I walked back, and as I grew closer to the tent, I saw the

cleaners hard at work. Trailers were packed up and all the expensive equipment secured away. Soon, we'd be done until next week. Evie was leaving the show, and already the carpenters were dismantling her workstation. I was about to head to the pub and our goodbye dinner with Evie when I caught a glimmer of orange rubber on the lawn in front of the big tent.

No wonder Sly hadn't had his ball with him. He'd dropped it here again. I went to fetch it, and as I bent down, I noticed the ball was in pieces. Someone had slashed it. I had a pretty good idea who. I glanced up, furious, and saw Peter Puddifoot's lawnmower parked at the edge of the field. There was no way he could've needed to mow the lawn again so soon. I thought that vicious man must've deliberately re-mowed that section so he could destroy that beautiful dog's beloved ball. I didn't get red-hot rages very often, but in that moment, a veil of crimson seemed to descend over my eyes. There was already tragedy in that house. How could anyone add more? Or was he only adding to pain he himself had created?

I headed straight into the pub, looking for my quarry. Most of the bakers were there, including Evie, who was finally relaxed and laughing over a glass of wine. As hard as it had been to have to leave the show, I thought she was relieved that her ordeal was over. The silver fox, Reginald McMahon, was sitting at a table with three men I thought might be locals and Bob Fielding, who had a tablet computer out and was showing it to the men. Looked like he was trying to sell more tires.

He was still bundled up and looked ill.

I thought you'd have to sell a lot of fireplace tools and iron garden accessories to be able to afford the fancy tires, but I gave the man full credit for trying to make another sale, especially as he still looked to be under the weather.

There was, however, no sign of my quarry. Much as it would have given me satisfaction to throw the pieces of shredded rubber right into Peter Puddifoot's face and humiliate him in public, I couldn't do it. He wasn't there.

Eve was behind the bar, and she called me over. "How are you feeling today, Poppy?" There was such significance in her tone, I wondered what she was referring to, and then I realized she was obliquely asking how I'd enjoyed my first visit with the coven. Right now, I couldn't even think about witch business unless there was a spell that would turn Peter Puddifoot into something unspeakable. Toad was much too good for him. Dung beetle was about right.

"Yes, it was all fine. Have you seen Peter Puddifoot? It's urgent."

Her eyebrows rose at that and, like me, she cast her gaze around the pub. "He's usually here on a Sunday afternoon. If he's not here, he's probably finishing up at the operations center. That's where they keep all the equipment." She gave me directions, and I thanked her and headed out before the baking show contestants pulled me into their group.

I left the pub and headed past the tent in the direction Eve had pointed me. I jumped a mile when a voice said, "What's your hurry, sunshine?"

I glanced around to make sure no one was in sight before answering. "Gerry. You scared me."

"Well, you're stomping along with murder in your eyes, so you're scaring me."

"It's that dreadful Peter Puddifoot." I told him what had

happened and showed him the pieces of ball I was still carrying.

Even Gerry looked shocked. "What kind of vile little man goes after a nice dog like that? He's not all there."

"When I'm done with him, he'll be a sorry mess, and I will personally make sure he buys Sly another ball."

I was walking so fast, I was almost past the tent. Gerry said, "Poppy. Wait. Don't go confronting the man who had the strongest motive to kill Arnold Bentley. What are you, crazy?"

I paused. He was right. I was crazy. Crazy with rage. I shook my head. "He won't kill me. Anyway, if he does, I just told Eve where I'm going, so he'll be caught red-handed."

He reached out and tried to grab my arm, but all I felt was a slight chill on my elbow. "Poppy. I can't follow you. And much as I'd like your company over here on the other side— think of the pranks we could play with two of us—you need to calm down and think this through." I didn't answer. I just kept walking. Finally, he yelled. "At least get your phone out so you can call the police if that madman attacks you."

Okay, he had a point. I pulled out my phone, punched in 999 and put it in my pocket where I could hit the button to connect the call if I had to.

The afternoon was drawing to a close, but I found the paved service road hidden from view behind some ornamental fencing. I looked back to wave goodbye to Gerry, who was hovering at the edge of the tent. I also took in that great hulking lawnmower at the side of the lawn, ready to destroy more harmless dog toys, and that infuriated me all over again. Puddifoot hadn't even bothered to put the mower away. What was he planning to do with it? Mow down the tent so no more annoying bakers would mess up his lawn?

Every time I thought of the joyful way Sly bounded after that ball, my anger surged. Gerry, meanwhile, was like a dog at the end of his leash, straining toward me. He kept calling out. "Poppy. It's not safe. Come back." But I ignored him, of course. Peter Puddifoot wouldn't dare hurt me. Besides, I had the protection spell, and just last week, when I had been threatened by Gordon, a tremendous surge of power had come over me. I would call on the power again if I needed to.

Now that I was surrounded by a coven of powerful witches, I no longer felt so alone. Peter Puddifoot would mess with me at his peril. Even as I had these powerful thoughts, I knew I'd be glad when the encounter was over and I had given the horrible gardener a piece of my mind. Even better, I'd ensure that Sly got a new ball.

At the end of the rough road was a clearing surrounded by trees. There wasn't much activity going on down here at the operations center. Everything was quiet. I didn't know where the gardener was and I couldn't see him, so I called out his name. I wasn't going to give him the dignity of calling out Mr. Puddifoot, and I certainly didn't feel chummy enough to call him Peter.

I stood there and yelled, "Peter Puddifoot." There was no answer. Was he hiding from me?

If he knew what was good for him, he would be. There was a garage housing tractors and farm equipment, another with a couple of old dusty trucks and a dented blue Volvo that had to be older than me. I wondered if one of those vehicles belonged to the gardener.

Behind the second garage was a hut that had a sign saying "Office" on the front door. I went forward, clutching the pieces of orange rubber in one hand and knocking with the other. I might be furious, but I was still British enough to knock before I entered.

I cursed myself for a fool that I hadn't asked Eve where he lived. If he wasn't in the pub or this hut, I'd have to keep looking.

There was no answer, but the door was slightly ajar. I heard voices inside. Was he ignoring me while chatting to another Broomewode employee? Or on the phone?

I stood there a minute until I realized the voice I was hearing was coming from a radio. I knocked once more and, assuming he was just ignoring me, I pushed the door open. I took a step inside, and a terrible feeling came over me. I felt dread and horror and fear. It was as powerful as a shove in the chest, and I stumbled a step back. Then I saw Peter Puddifoot. He was lying facedown on the floor. I called out his name, but I was almost certain that intensity of emotions I had experienced was a compilation of his final moments. He was dead.

In the time it took me to accept that fact, I also took in the gash in the back of his head. On the floor beside him, looking almost as out of place as a dead body, was a fancy black iron fire poker.

I didn't need to read the bloodstained card to know that it was forged by Reginald McMahon and sold at the gift shop by the pub.

As much as I hated to touch the man, I had to be absolutely certain he was dead. I crept forward, nearly gagging at the smell, and checked the pulse in his wrist. There wasn't one. Almost worse, if anything could be worse, he wasn't quite cold.

I scuttled backward out of the hut and then, taking my phone in my shaking hand, completed the call.

I told the emergency operator what I'd found and where, and she told me to stay right where I was. I understood that it was the right thing to do, but the thought of standing here alone when there was a murderer somewhere in the area was terrifying.

I would stay here as instructed, but I couldn't handle standing here alone. Luckily, we bakers had shared phone numbers amongst ourselves. I scanned through, wondering who I could call, and I immediately saw Hamish. Of course. Solid, reliable, Scottish cop Hamish. I didn't want to alarm him or the others, so I simply asked him to meet me at the shed by the operations center. "And if you could come immediately, I'd really appreciate it."

He didn't argue or ask foolish questions. "I'm on my way."

Even so, it seemed like a very long time before he arrived, though it took three minutes. I knew, because I kept watching my phone second by second.

I imagined he'd come alone, but when he arrived, Gaurav was with him.

No doubt they'd been sitting together when he got the call and Gaurav insisted on coming along. I couldn't worry about that now. Briefly, I told them both what I'd discovered.

Hamish immediately went into police mode. "You called it in?"

"Yes. Emergency services are on their way."

"You're sure he's dead?"

I shuddered. "Positive."

He nodded, then stepped toward the hut. He pulled his

sweatshirt sleeve down over his hand and used it to nudge the door open. He didn't step inside but examined the same view I'd recently seen. He came back. "Poor sod. He wouldn't have known what hit him."

"I guess that's good," Gaurav said. "But I was so sure he'd killed Arnold Bentley."

Hamish nodded as we stood there in the gathering gloom. "He definitely had the motive, the means, and the opportunity. But if he killed Arnold Bentley, then who killed him?"

"Or did the same person kill both of them? And if so, why?"

I sighed. "I didn't like the man, and he was horrible to Sly, but that's an awful way to die."

I shivered, in cold and reaction, and without saying a word, Gaurav slipped off his woolen coat and put it over my shoulders. It felt warm and as comforting as a hug.

It wasn't long until the police arrived. First an ambulance, and then, inevitably, Detective Inspector Hembly and Sergeant Lane.

The paramedics went in first and confirmed that Peter Puddifoot was dead. Then, before anyone else was allowed in, the detectives put on crime scene boots and gloves and entered the hut.

DI Hembly came out alone a few minutes later. Very briefly I told him what I had found. He nodded and asked me to wait at the inn until they could take my statement.

I longed to be back at the warm and cozy inn, but before I left, I wanted to tell them about the poker. "There's something you should know. The fire poker that was used to kill Peter Puddifoot—" I paused and then continued, "at least I think it's the murder weapon. It's got his blood and some of his hair on it."

The older man nodded. "Forensics will confirm, but it seems the likely murder weapon. Have you seen it before?"

I nodded. "They sell them at the gift shop here. The blacksmith who makes them, Reginald McMahon, is in the pub right now."

His face didn't change expression, but it shifted slightly. In DI Hembly, this was akin to a normal person's jaw dropping open in shock. "Reginald McMahon. We met him today. He came to check on Susan Bentley while we were there."

"I believe they are close friends," I said, not wishing to accuse one of my sister witches of murder but also not prepared to shield her if she was guilty.

He glanced up in the direction of the inn. "I'll be up shortly. I think it might be useful to have a word with Mr. McMahon."

Hamish said, "The baking contestants are all at the pub having a final meal before we leave. Can Poppy join us?"

"Yes, of course. Just, please, none of you say anything about this."

He didn't need to worry. I'd like to wipe the gruesome discovery out of my memory. I certainly didn't want to talk about it. I turned and then realized I was still holding the pieces of Sly's ball. I had no idea if it was relevant, but I told DI Hembly about the shredded ball and that I was certain Peter Puddifoot had deliberately run over it with a lawnmower. "That's why I was here," I told him. "I was planning to give Mr. Puddifoot a piece of my mind."

He held out his hand for the pieces of ball, and I gratefully handed them over. He looked down at the shreds of orange rubber in his palm. "Very fond of that dog, is Susan Bentley."

I nodded. Was he thinking what I was thinking? If Reginald McMahon had been willing to kill Arnold Bentley in order to be with his wife, it didn't seem implausible that he might kill Peter Puddifoot in revenge for his treatment of Sly.

CHAPTER 14

$\mathcal{W}$e walked back to the inn, and who did I find but my lovely Gateau, chasing a moth fluttering around a lighted window. She meowed when she saw me and came over to be petted.

"Hello, sweet thing," I murmured. "Where on earth have you been? I haven't seen you for ages." She followed us back into the pub, and I returned Gaurav's coat and told them I'd be down in a minute. I needed to wash up. Gateau looked tired, so I took her upstairs with me. Naturally, Gerry was there, pacing. "Oh, Poppy, I'm so glad to see you." He looked me over critically. "You don't look so good. Did the dog-hater attack you?"

"No. Someone got there before me. He was dead."

He settled himself in the armchair while Gateau jumped onto the bed and immediately curled up and went to sleep. I wanted to do that too. With the covers over my head.

"Dead?" He looked around. "He'd better not hang around here. I didn't like him in life, and I'm definitely not keen on being mates now."

"I don't think he's still around. I haven't seen him, anyway."

"How did he snuff it, then?"

I told him about the poker to the back of the head. "So, did you hear anything eavesdropping in the pub last night?"

"Not much. Bob Fielding, the tire salesman, was boasting about a big sale to Lord Frome, but he has to wait until Monday for a check. That's why he's still here. He's not wasting his time, either. Even though he should be in bed with that cold, he's endlessly trying to flog his wheels. If not to the film crew, then to the locals."

I nodded. I'd noticed that, too.

"Did you happen to hear anything about Reginald McMahan?"

"He wasn't there last night. It was a funny night altogether. Jonathon was there, having a pint with the lads, but kept looking at his watch, then suddenly looked out the window and headed off. If you ask me, he's got a bird in the area."

Or a coven.

"It was mostly blokes in the pub last night. The women all seemed to be somewhere else."

I freshened up as quickly as I could. I'd only touched Peter Puddifoot's wrist, but the whole experience made my flesh crawl. I took a quick shower and dressed in jeans and a comfy red sweater that felt both warm and cheerful. I needed to pack up, as we had to check out, but I still needed dinner and, of course, there was my upcoming interview with the police.

By the time I got back down to the pub, most of the other contestants had left. Florence was pouting again and said that

Evie had waited to say goodbye, but she had to leave to catch her train. In fact, they'd all gone but Florence, Gaurav, and Hamish, who were sitting around a small circular table by the fireplace, suitcases by their sides.

I was impressed to see that Hamish's cold had completely disappeared. I wondered if Elspeth would teach me to make healing tonics. It seemed a better gift than being able to communicate with the dearly departed.

The sound of laughter and glasses clinking caused me to look around. Sitting around a large oak table, I spied Elspeth and Jonathon with Jilly, Arty and some of the crew, including Gina. Until I saw that big grin of hers, nattering away and playing with a strand of her hair, I hadn't realized how much I'd missed my best friend this weekend. I'd been so caught up with the Bentleys and Elspeth's magic circle that I'd only managed to see Gina when she was doing my makeup, and there had been too many people around for us to talk properly. I wished so much that I could tell her everything about my newfound witch status, but I didn't know how or even if it was allowed. The last thing I wanted was to upset Elspeth or do anything that might get me in trouble with my new sisters.

Reginald McMahan and Bob Fielding were still talking cars with the two locals I'd seen them with earlier. Bob Fielding even had a racing cap on his head. It looked like the world's most boring conversation to me, but they seemed riveted. "You won't be sorry," the salesman was telling Reg. "Those tires will last many years, even in this tough terrain. Top of the line." He shivered and pulled his sweatshirt tighter around him.

I was torn. Florence, Hamish and Gaurav were on one side of the pub, Elspeth and Gina on the other. There was so much I wanted to share with all of them—and I needed Gaurav's help. But my old friendship had to come first for a moment. I went to Gina's table and wrapped her in a bear hug.

"Pops!" she exclaimed, laughing, "Where have you been all day?"

I couldn't tell her about finding Peter Puddifoot or my suspicions about how Arnold had died. I needed to play this next scene carefully, so I only said I'd been out walking. It was true enough.

Gina frowned. "Pops. You're so bad at lying. What aren't you telling me? Is it a man?" She glanced over at where Hamish and Gaurav sat and then back at me with raised eyebrows.

"No."

Then she grabbed my wrist. "Wait, I saw you head up the path to the manor earlier. You're not ogling the lord of the manor, are you?"

"Who, Benedict? No." As if.

She looked unconvinced. Then leaned closer. "If you were super rich, I'd say go for it, but his last girlfriend was Lady Ophelia Wren."

I felt my eyes widen. "The celebrity doctor?"

Lady Ophelia Wren was famous for giving humanitarian medical aid all over the world. That she was also gorgeous and titled only added to her allure. The press loved her, and so did half the men in the UK. Probably the world. And she'd dated Benedict? "What happened?"

She leaned closer and dropped her voice. "I heard she wanted to get married and he shied away." She shrugged. "You'd be surprised what secrets I hear in the makeup chair."

Florence called me from across the room, so I was saved by the tinkle of her theatrical voice. "We'll talk later," I said to Gina. "I promise."

When I reached Florence she said, "We've been dying to share Gaurav's findings with you."

He looked mildly pleased with himself. "I found the list of all the plaintiffs in the class-action suit. I've also got a list of how much money they lost." He pushed his computer screen toward me. "You asked me to give you the geographical locations, and as far as I could, I grouped them according to how close they live to Broomewode."

"Nice work." I was impressed. Naturally, Lord and Lady Frome's names were at the top of his list. They hadn't been part of the class-action suit, interestingly enough. However, if Benedict had told me the truth, Arnold Bentley had warned Lord and Lady Frome to get out early and so they hadn't lost much. Presumably, that resulted in his getting the farm for low rent.

I read through the list carefully. There was no McMahan listed. But then, he'd lived in London at the time. I began reading the names of those who'd lived closer to London.

I must have made a sound, for Gaurav said, "What? You've found something? I searched and couldn't find a connection."

"I'm not sure," I answered him slowly. But I had a hunch.

The two detectives came in just then. Sgt. Lane was wearing dark denim jeans and a crisp white shirt. His brown hair tumbled forward as he ran a hand through his locks and looked around the room. DI Hembly looked as formal as ever in pressed navy trousers and blazer.

"Ah, Poppy," Hembly said, approaching our table. "Are you ready to give a statement?"

Florence looked like she'd choked on a lemon. "Statement? What kind of statement?"

Before anyone answered her, I said softly, "I think I know who did it. Would you let me try something?"

The two detectives exchanged a glance. Adam shrugged. It was obviously DI Hembly's call.

I swallowed hard. It was a bit like baking under pressure. I had the ingredients, and I thought everything would go together all right, but at any moment, the whole structure could fall apart.

Susan Bentley came quietly into the pub, Sly at her side like a shadow.

"I hope you know what you're doing," DI Hembly said. I took that as unenthusiastic permission. I hoped I knew what I was doing, too.

I stood up, feeling more shaky than when I'd flipped my upside-down cake yesterday. And that had turned out okay. This would too.

"Excuse me, can I have everyone's attention, please?" I said it as loud as I could, but after a slight pause, the chatting and laughter continued.

"Hey," a new voice bellowed. It was Eve. "The next person who interrupts Poppy will be banned from this bar until further notice."

Well, that quieted them immediately. She gave me an encouraging nod and held my gaze long enough for me to feel her strength adding to mine. I turned, and there was Elspeth looking at me, calm and serene. Even Jonathon seemed to add to my sense of control.

"As you all know, Arnold Bentley died tragically yesterday," I began. "And his death wasn't an accident."

There were mutters of surprise, disbelief.

"He was murdered, by someone in this room."

Reginald McMahan stood. "Sorry, I've got orders to finish tonight. Somebody fill me in tomorrow." He took one step toward the doorway.

"Stay where you are, Reg." I hadn't seen Benedict come in, but he sounded firm and commanding. My goodness, *everyone* was here.

The blacksmith hesitated, then sat and took another drink of his beer. His color was heightened.

I had not rehearsed this at all, and I was starting to choke under pressure. Hamish raised an eyebrow at me, and that gave me an idea. "Hamish, could you stand up, please?"

He did, looking completely mystified.

"Hamish is a contestant on our show, but he's also a police officer in his day job." I could feel a shiver of emotion. Curiosity, irritation, and the first stirrings of fear.

"I hate to ask for your help when you're so sick with that cold, Hamish." I said this so loud the bees at Broomewode Farm would hear me if they were listening.

He frowned momentarily, confused at the direction this was going, but he played along. "I'm not sick anymore. That medicine you gave me worked a treat."

I could have kissed him.

I looked over at Bob Fielding, sitting beside Reg, still bundled up in coat and scarf and cap and looking downright miserable. "My magic healing tonic didn't work so well for you, though, did it, Mr. Fielding?" I said, projecting my voice across the room.

He looked surprised to be addressed. "I'm not feeling as poorly as I did, thank you."

This was the moment. I nearly lost my nerve, but Sly moved from beside Susan and rubbed his head against my calf. Elspeth regarded me with great calmness, and Jonathon looked supportive.

"But you're clearly still feeling the cold, aren't you? It's very warm in here, with the fire going, and yet you're bundled up like it's zero degrees. I'm surprised you had any success, Mr. Fielding, selling your tires to Broomewode Hall yesterday. With that stinking cold."

"You do take the most extraordinary interest in other people's affairs," Benedict said. Susan whispered something to him, and he rolled his eyes and leaned against the doorjamb. I wished he'd go away. He was making me even more nervous than the detective inspector, who was looking pretty annoyed that I was putting on this floor show. Still, DI Hembly obviously thought that the quicker he indulged me, the sooner he could get back to his Sunday tea.

"It's a common name, Bob Fielding," I continued. "A colleague did some research on you. He's thinking of getting a hot car and some new tires, you see." I pointed at Gaurav, who looked quite astonished to find himself in the market for new wheels.

"He discovered a Robert A. Fielding."

The man flinched, tightening his scarf as though he were chilled, even though his face looked red and hot. "He was one of the people who invested their life savings into Arnold Bentley's company. I believe that Bob Fielding lost nearly all his money."

Gaurav corrected me. "Ten pence on the pound, that's all they got back, the people who'd invested their life savings in Arnold Bentley's company. Just ten pence on the pound.

You'd have to sell an awful lot of tires to make that kind of money back."

"Well, as you say, it's a common name," the man said. "Now, if you'll excuse me, I have to be in Truro tomorrow, so I've a very long drive ahead. I must get on my way."

"Would you take off your scarf, Mr. Fielding?" I said with a confidence I was faking so hard. The entire pub fell silent. All eyes were on me and Bob. I could feel the sweat gathering at the nape of my neck, but I needed to have faith in myself and stand my ground.

Bob rose, looking annoyed. "I don't know who you are, but—"

DI Hembly cleared his throat. "Miss Wilkinson is cooperating with the local police, Mr. Fielding. Kindly do as she says, unless you'd feel more comfortable down at the station?"

Bob looked around the room with a beseeching expression. "Oh, this is ridiculous. Is it a crime to come down with a cold in Somerset?"

DI Hembly chuckled. "If it was, most of us would spend half the year in jail." He paused. "Your scarf, sir? We don't want to be all night."

With an irritated shrug, Bob Fielding unwound the scarf from around his neck. I counted four angry red welts. "Hives," he said before anyone else could speak. "It's a nervous condition."

"Not hives," Susan Bentley said, stepping forward. "Bee stings. I know the look of them well." She got closer. "They got in your hair, too. I can see the welts underneath your cap."

Florence gasped. "Oh. My. God," she said in a disbelieving

tone.

"Take the cap off, sir," DI Hembly commanded. "And your jacket."

Bob turned beet-red. He began to mumble in protest, but then Sgt. Lane took a step toward. "Like the detective inspector said, we can continue this down at the station."

Bob Fielding looked around the pub, but everyone was staring. He must have known he couldn't argue his way out of doing as I'd asked. He removed his cap and, reluctantly, his jacket. Florence gasped again. Bob Fielding was covered in bright welts that perfectly matched the shameful expression on his face.

I turned and looked at Susan. I knew she wanted the mystery of her husband's death to be solved, but I hadn't planned to do it right in front of her. Why hadn't she stayed quietly at the farmhouse? Because of me, Susan was now face-to-face with Arnold's murderer. I couldn't even imagine the emotions that must be coursing through her body. But her tired face had a neutral expression etched across it. She was watching the events unfold with an extraordinary calm. Sly moved back to her side. He seemed to always know who needed him most.

Bob Fielding tried to brazen it out. "All right. I got stung. I was up at Broomewode Hall, and when I walked past the farm, there was a great swarm of bees. Didn't want to make a fuss, that's all."

Benedict spoke. "And yet, I was up and down that path all day. I didn't get stung. Nor did anyone else."

Susan Bentley gave Sly a quick stroke and then came toward Bob. "I can give you something that will soothe the pain of those stings," she said, surprising all of us.

"What?" Florence cried out.

"He killed your husband," Eve reminded her, leaning across the bar.

Susan smiled sadly. "I know. But my husband lost all his money. Everything he ever worked for. I know what it feels like to lose everything. It's a very lonely place." She slipped off her backpack and brought out a small pot of salve. She gave it to the red-faced man. "Dab it on the welts three times a day. It should do the trick."

"Thank you," he said. "I didn't mean to. I feel. I feel—"

"You should feel terrible, you murderer," Florence said, shaking her long tresses in disgust.

There was a silence. And then he spoke. "You don't understand. How could you? I worked all my life. Saved like they tell you to. Invested for a comfortable retirement. And he lost it all." He looked at Gaurav. "You're right. Ten pence on the pound isn't much, and we had to pay the lawyer out of that. But Arnold's rich friends were all right, though. Their lawyers fought hard and dirty. Arnold made enough money off our backs to retire in luxury. Me? I'll be working till I drop, and so will the missus."

I caught Eve's eye, and she shook her head. We both knew that Bob Fielding wasn't going to be working another day for a long, long time. Not like he was used to, anyway.

"So I tracked Arnold Bentley down. I went to the farm to try and talk to him. Tell him he had to find me the money. I was only asking for what I was owed. Said he didn't have it. That he'd lost all his money too. Liar. I was furious."

"But how did you know Mr. Bentley was allergic to bees?" DI Hembly asked. Sgt. Lane was busily taking notes.

"I heard him and the old gardener going at it hammer

and tong, having a shouting match right outside that window when I first arrived."

It was the same fight I'd overheard, and Arnold Bentley had shouted to all the world how deathly allergic he was.

"I nearly laughed when I saw how easy it would be. I waited until his wife was out with the dog and then I knocked on the door, pretending to be the gardener. I'm not a bad mimic, and he was too angry to listen carefully. I called out that I was going to prune the hedges before he even answered the door."

"Arnold came running out of the house and around the side where the hedges and the hives were. But by the time he realized it was me, he'd already been stung. You see, I knocked down the beehive before I even started yelling. He ran right into the trap I'd set him. He reached in his pocket for an EpiPen, but I snatched it out of his hands and dragged him down to the swarm. Then I left him there."

Susan's eyes filled with tears.

Bob looked down at his feet, as if the enormity of what he'd done had only just hit. "He took everything from us, he did. Everything."

"But that wasn't your only attempt on his life, was it?" He glanced up at me, as though having trouble hearing my words. "You knocked one of the great stones off the top of the tower, thinking it was him out there, picking gooseberries."

"Tower? What tower?"

"Oh, come on. You've already confessed to murdering Arnold Bentley. Admitting to an attempt on my life won't change anything." It would make me feel better, though, since I'd been the one who nearly ended up flattened.

"I don't know what you're talking about. I was at the farm, not the manor house." He looked so genuinely confused, I wondered if it was possible he hadn't been responsible for my near miss with the Grim Reaper. But if it wasn't him, then who had knocked the stone off? Could it really have been an accident?

"When did you know that Peter Puddifoot the gardener had seen you kill Arnold Bentley?" I asked in a voice that was a lot more in control now that he'd already confessed.

He glanced at Reginald McMahan and then at me. "Don't know what you're talking about."

"Oh, come on. Peter Puddifoot saw you, or maybe he simply made a lucky guess." I thought of that vile dog-kicker. What might he have done if he suspected Bob Fielding of murder? Not gone to the police. I bet he'd have tried to turn the situation to his advantage. "Did he want a payoff to keep his mouth shut?"

He let out a breath and scratched one of the welts as though the itching was unbearable. "More than a payoff. He wanted Susan Bentley dead."

"What?" This from Susan herself.

"He knew I didn't have anything but a guilty conscience. He said he'd keep quiet if I did away with you, too."

"But why?" Susan asked, looking around.

"The farm," Benedict answered her. "He felt he should have had Broomewode Farm when his father died. He may have been right, but my father had other ideas. I think it became an obsession with him to get it back. He was always trying to make trouble for Arnold. Anything he could do to get rid of them, he would."

I wondered if it had been Peter Puddifoot who'd nearly

killed me, mistaking me for Susan. Unfortunately, unless he came back as a ghost, I wouldn't be able to ask him.

"Where is Pud?" Eve asked, glancing around. "He should be arrested."

"Peter Puddifoot is dead. Murdered earlier today." DI Hembly looked over at Reg. "And I believe the murder weapon was one of your fire pokers, Mr. McMahan."

The blacksmith rose to his feet, looking as fiery as his own forge. "What are you suggesting?"

"How might one of your hand-forged pokers end up beside the body?"

Reg looked around. "They sell the pokers here, at the gift shop. Tell them, Eve."

"They do. Yes."

"You don't seriously think I'd use my own poker to kill a man? Might as well leave a hand-signed note saying I did it."

"We'll need to see who bought a fire poker recently. Or if any are missing."

Reg glared at Bob Fielding. "I am canceling my order for new tires." And he moved, going to stand beside Susan.

Bob Fielding sat quietly for a minute, staring into his beer, then he looked up. "You won't find a receipt. I took the poker when the saleswoman was busy with another customer. I took it on impulse. I knew I couldn't kill Susan Bentley. My only option seemed to be to kill Peter Puddifoot. He was a vile creature. I'm not sorry."

"But are you sorry you tried to frame me?" Reg asked, sounding pretty angry.

"That wasn't my intention. I didn't know you were the blacksmith until this evening. And it was a bit late by then."

CHAPTER 15

Susan Bentley leaned against Reg as DI Hembly and
Sgt. Lane read Bob Fielding his rights. It was
strange how the words had already become so familiar to me.
"You do not have to say anything, but it may harm your
defense if you do not mention when questioned something
which you may rely on in court." As I watched Bob hang his
head and offer up his wrists to DI Hembly for cuffing, I had a
horrible sense of déjà vu. Like Gordon last week, Bob
Fielding seemed to feel like he was well within his rights to
kill someone who'd aggrieved him. First it was over love, and
now money. Like Gordon, Bob's speech had been calm and
collected, as if he was a rational human being and was now
prepared to accept his fate. DI Hembly walked him out of
the pub.

Gina stood and rushed over to my side. She put her arm
around my shoulder and whispered, "So you're some kind of
Baking Killer Catcher now, hmm?" she said, in awe. "Is there
no end to your talents?" I knew she was trying to lighten the
mood, but I couldn't bring myself to smile. I caught Elspeth's

eye, and she gave me an approving nod. I touched my amethyst necklace and nodded back. I certainly had been protected from the moment she gave it to me, and maybe that security had given me the confidence to pursue the mystery of Arnold's death. I had so much to be thankful to Elspeth for.

I turned to look at Susan. She'd averted her eyes during Bob's arrest, concentrating instead on stroking Sly. I was still perplexed and kind of stunned by her reaction to Bob's confession. Reg shook his head and then said, in a distressed tone, "He used my hand-crafted art as a murder weapon."

Susan put a comforting hand on his arm. "But in a way he was trying to protect me."

Gaurav jumped up and said he was honored to have been my colleague and help send that murderer to justice. I was astonished. I never would have imagined that Gaurav would transform from shy and retiring scientist to outspoken crime-busting sidekick. Clearly, I still had a lot to learn about people and the heights they could climb, as well as the depths they could sink to.

"I've got to get back to Birmingham tonight, Poppy," Gaurav said, "and if I don't leave now, I'll miss my train." He stuck out his hand. "It was good being partners with you this weekend." I shook his hand vigorously. What a stand-up guy.

Florence and Hamish waved him off. Hamish turned to me. "You should think about police work," Hamish said. "You've a knack for it."

"Thanks for the compliment, but I should probably leave the real police work to the professionals." I glanced at Elspeth. "I'd rather have a knack for healing."

Hamish breathed in deeply, and I could hear that his cold

was gone. "Yes, whatever was in that potion you gave me, it was magic." I didn't dare look at Elspeth as he thanked me, and then he, too, left the pub. The weekend was finally coming to an end.

Florence wrapped me in a bear hug. "I can't wait to see you next week, Poppy. And let's hope all we have to worry about is our baking and no more murders." She pulled back and glanced out the window in the direction of the manor house. "I hope Broomewode Hall isn't cursed," Florence said darkly.

"Oh now, now," Elspeth admonished. I hadn't even noticed her approach us. "No such thing. Broomewode is a beautiful place, not somewhere to be afraid of. We've just been unlucky, but all that's over now. You need to put all this fear behind you and get ready to bake your socks off next weekend. That's all you need to worry about."

"I'll say," Florence replied. She made a grand sweeping motion with her hand and curtseyed. "Adieu, dear friends. London calls." I giggled as she made her grand exit.

Elspeth turned to me. "That was quite some detective work."

I lowered my voice. "I've been wondering if perhaps it might be part of my powers. An intuitive of sorts, for mysterious deaths. Could it be linked to being a water witch? Or am I getting ahead of myself?"

Elspeth assured me that a growing intuition, of any kind, was a sure sign that the energy vortex of Broomewode Hall was working its own magic.

"But I don't feel like I'm getting any closer to solving the mystery of my birth parents—" I stopped myself. Was that strictly true? I recalled the vision of the woman that had appeared to me in the bathtub and her warning. Even though I'd never it heard it before, the more I remembered that night, the more convinced I was that the voice was familiar. I recognized it somehow. And then I remembered the image of the smiling man at the witches' circle. I recounted these sightings to Elspeth. "What do you think it means? *Am* I getting closer?"

"An increase in your visions is certainly a step in the right direction, Poppy," Elspeth said gently. "Be patient. And practice your protection spell. As much as I'd like the show to be smooth sailing from now on, I have a feeling that it might not be that easy. I don't want you coming to any harm." She laid a slim, elegant hand on my shoulder, and I felt a zing of power that went through my arm. "And I don't want any mishaps in the kitchen, either." I felt she was making it clear I had to work to ensure my passage into the next round. I couldn't afford to rest on my laurels after winning one competition. The remaining bakers were all amazing.

I gulped. No pressure then.

I gathered my things, ready to head back to my little cottage. I said goodbye to Susan, promising to come visit her when I returned next Friday. Maybe I'd bring her some of my practice bakes from the week, some comforting rich coffee cake or some biscuits to dip into tea. I wanted her to know that I was going to take my newfound sisterhood seriously. Understanding more about the coven was key to understanding my true identity as a witch and, with any luck, more about who my parents were. With Katie Donegal now recuperating in Ireland, my cunning plan to grill her for more information about people who'd lived in the village now amounted to zilch. And I'd yet to find another way to get inside Broomewode Hall. Not for the first time, I wondered if something, or someone, was conspiring to keep me away.

I glanced at Benedict, who was currently stroking Sly.

"Did you get your letter?" Eve asked me.

"What letter?"

"Oh, those chambermaids. Not a brain between them. I asked Sarah to make sure and take it to your room. Now where could it be? Ah, here it is," Eve said, handing me an envelope with my name written in neat black capital letters on the front.

I tore open the envelope so quickly, I gave myself a paper cut.

DEAREST POPPY,

You are in terrible danger. You shouldn't be here. I'm begging you: Please leave Broomewode Manor. Do something to get yourself voted off of the show next week. Otherwise I fear it will be too late. Please heed my words.

I GULPED. Blood pounded in my ears, and I felt my heart rate quicken. I shook my head, dumfounded. Who on earth would send me this? And why leave it unsigned? I looked around the room for anyone watching me. Was this some kind of sick joke?

"Goodness, Poppy," Eve said. "What is it? You've gone the most terrific shade of white. It's like I'm looking at a ghost."

A ghost. Could this be Gerry's doing? But Gerry couldn't hold a pen. Another contestant who saw me as a threat? But I felt like they were all my friends.

"Poppy?' Eve said again, breaking the train of my racing thoughts.

I took a breath. I wasn't ready to cause any more alarm. The cast, crew, and staff here at the inn had been through enough already without me adding a cryptic warning note to the mix. "Oh, it's nothing. Just a message about keys to my cottage," I mumbled. Wow. In my shock, I couldn't even think of a good lie.

Luckily, Jonathon was motioning to Eve for some more drinks, so I didn't have to explain any further. She kissed my cheek and said she'd see me next week.

I tried to calm my unsteady breath and regain control of my whirring mind. So I'd received a warning about being in danger—it wasn't even the first one of the week. The woman in my vision had said the same thing. In a way, I was being protected, even if it also felt a bit like being threatened. What was worse: being spoken to from some other dimension or receiving some creepy note?

I felt something at my feet, and then Sly was pushing against my knee. I bent and nuzzled into his warm coat, wrapping my arms around his neck. "I won't forget what you did for me this week, boy," I whispered into his ear. "You'll be getting some treats of your own next week, too. And a new ball. Just don't abandon me next weekend—it seems like I need all the protection I can get."

I heard an angry meow. And then felt something butting against my side. I twisted round, and Gateau was looking up at me, furious. "I'm so sorry, my little puss. Don't think I forgot about you and the role you played either. Whether you like it or not, you and Sly are a good team." Her green eyes were pools of distaste, communicating the sentiment *I don't think so, silly human* remarkably well. I picked up the little fur ball, and she nestled into the crook of my arm. She didn't hold grudges either.

"Come on," Reg said to Susan. "It's been an emotional day. Let's get you home."

After they left, Benedict came up to me. "And did you make it through to the next round?"

Knowing that the two judges and several of the crew were listening, I said, "I'm afraid I can't discuss any details of the show."

His lips twitched. "It's all right. I signed a non-disclosure agreement, too." The twitch turned into the hint of a smile.

"Well, okay, yes, I'm through to the next round."

He nodded, his eyes holding mine. "See you next week, then."

A Note from Nancy

Dear Reader,

Thank you for reading The Great Witches Baking Show series. I am so grateful for all the enthusiasm this series has received. I have more stories about Poppy planned for the future.

I hope you'll consider leaving a review and please tell your friends who like cozy mysteries and culinary adventures.

Review on Amazon, Goodreads or BookBub.

Your support is appreciated. Turn the page for Poppy's recipe for Gooseberry Upside-Down Cake with Raspberry Kisses.

Join my newsletter at nancywarren.net to hear about my new releases and special offers.

I hope to see you in my private Facebook Group. It's a lot of fun. www.facebook.com/groups/NancyWarrenKnitwits

Until next time,
Happy Reading,

Nancy

POPPY'S RECIPE FOR GOOSEBERRY UPSIDE-DOWN CAKE WITH RASPBERRY KISSES

So here you have it. The winning recipe for the fruit cake round! Nothing could compare to the delight I felt when Elspeth and Jonathon announced that I'd won this challenge. And just because you're such lovely readers, I'm going to share my recipe with you here. I can promise you that this gooseberry and elderflower delight with mini raspberry meringues will win you the heart of anyone who takes a bite. Make sure that the gooseberries are in season when you make this cake—it's what will help you achieve the right balance of tartness with the sweet and sumptuous raspberry meringues. It's difficult to give an exact bake time for meringues, as it very much depends on your oven. Just keep an eye on them until they're done.

Adding a little whipped cream to the whole thing could be a naughty treat, too. When it comes to cakes, sometimes more is more.

This recipe will serve a hungry ten people.

Ingredients:

Gooseberry layer:

0.9 oz. honey (try to find some from "contented bees")

3.5 oz. gooseberries

Sponge:

2 (happy) eggs

4 oz. sugar

4 oz. self-rising flour (or regular flour with 1 teaspoon baking powder added)

4 oz. unsalted butter

Raspberry Kisses

3 large egg whites

5.3 oz. caster (super fine) sugar

2.5 tablespoons of freeze-dried raspberries

<u>Method:</u>

1. Firstly, you know that you'll have to grease a cake tin and line it with baking parchment before any of the fun stuff begins. In this case, you'll be needing a flat 8-inch cake tin, and you'll need to grease it again once the parchment is in place. Nothing worse than sticky gooseberries stuck to your tin.

2. Now cover the bottom of the tin with a good old heap of the honey. Place an even layer of gooseberries on top. This might be a bit finicky, but it's worth them not overlapping too much.

3. Now it's time to make your sponge. Add all the ingredients to a processor and blend.

4. Bake at 180 C/350 F for 40 minutes until the sponge turns a lovely golden brown.

5. Meanwhile, you can make a start on your raspberry kisses. Heat the oven to 100 C/215 F.

6. Line two baking sheets with greaseproof paper.

7. Beat the egg whites using an electric whisk or stand mixer in a large, spotlessly clean bowl until soft peaks form.

8. Add the sugar gradually, a tablespoon at a time, whisking well after each addition, until all the sugar has been added.

9. Continue to whisk the meringue for a few minutes more until it is very thick and glossy and forms stiff peaks when you lift the whisk out of the bowl.

10. In a pestle and mortar, grind the freeze-dried raspberries to a fine powder, then pass it through a sieve to remove the seeds. Now add it your meringue mix.

11. Fit a piping bag with a large plain or star nozzle, and then fill the bag with the meringue and twist the top closed. Use a little meringue mix to stick the greaseproof paper to the baking trays (this makes it easier to pipe) and pipe small "kisses," slightly spaced apart on the trays.

12. Bake for about 35 minutes, but be aware that they could take longer depending on your oven. They are ready when they can be lifted off the paper in one piece—if the bottom comes away, they aren't ready yet.

13. Make sure that the cake has cooled, and then carefully turn it out onto a plate. Decorate around the base with your finished raspberry kisses, and there you have it—an award-winning cake!

Bon appétit!

A Rolling Scone - Book 3

Toni Diamond Mysteries

Toni is a successful saleswoman for Lady Bianca Cosmetics in this series of humorous cozy mysteries. Along with having an eye for beauty and a head for business, Toni's got a nose for trouble and she's never shy about following her instincts, even when they lead to murder.

Frosted Shadow - Book 1

Ultimate Concealer - Book 2

Midnight Shimmer - Book 3

A Diamond Choker For Christmas - A Toni Diamond Mysteries Novella

The Almost Wives Club

An enchanted wedding dress is a matchmaker in this series of romantic comedies where five runaway brides find out who the best men really are!

The Almost Wives Club: Kate - Book 1

Second Hand Bride - Book 2

Bridesmaid for Hire - Book 3

The Wedding Flight - Book 4

If the Dress Fits - Book 5

Take a Chance series

Meet the Chance family, a cobbled together family of eleven kids who are all grown up and finding their ways in life and love.

Kiss a Girl in the Rain - Book 1

Iris in Bloom - Book 2

Blueprint for a Kiss - Book 3

Every Rose - Book 4

Love to Go - Book 5

The Sheriff's Sweet Surrender - Book 6

The Daisy Game - Book 7

Chance Encounter - Prequel

Take a Chance Box Set - Prequel and Books 1-3

For a complete list of books, check out Nancy's website at nancywarren.net

ABOUT THE AUTHOR

Nancy Warren is the USA Today Bestselling author of more than 70 novels. She's originally from Vancouver, Canada, though she tends to wander and has lived in England, Italy and California at various times. While living in Oxford she dreamed up The Vampire Knitting Club. She currently splits her time between Bath, UK, where she often pretends she's Jane Austen. Or at least a character in a Jane Austen novel, and Victoria, British Columbia where she enjoys living by the ocean. Favorite moments include being the answer to a crossword puzzle clue in Canada's National Post newspaper, being featured on the front page of the New York Times when her book Speed Dating launched Harlequin's NASCAR series, and being nominated three times for Romance Writers of America's RITA award. She has an MA in Creative Writing from Bath Spa University. She's an avid hiker, loves chocolate and most of all, loves to hear from readers! The best way to stay in touch is to sign up for Nancy's newsletter at www.nancywarren.net.

To learn more about Nancy and her books
www.nancywarren.net

Made in the USA
Las Vegas, NV
10 July 2021

26245666R00118